CYNTHIA MELTON

The Others

Nightfall, Book Three

Cynthia Melton

1

I watched through the monitor screen as more cameras were strategically placed around our compound. Several now pointed straight in the direction of Soriah. I wanted to know every step President Cane and his sidekick Sharon made.

"Helicopter," I said through the men's earpieces.

They ducked into hiding until the aircraft passed, then resumed their work. Normally, monitoring the cameras was left to Lars and Dayton, but on occasion, I took a shift to study the layout of the city and plan how best to take down the army. So far, we'd only managed to thin them out a little at a time, nibbling at their ankles like the rats that roamed the city.

If we could destroy the army, we'd deal Soriah a blow the white city might never recover from. I glanced at the monitor showing the area around the army's camp. We couldn't get close enough to see the actual camp, although we had people working on increasing the distance.

Eb shuffled into the control room, leaning heavily on his cane. "I found the blueprints behind one of the energy panels."

I grinned and called for Lars over the loudspeaker before turning to the old man. "Was I right?"

"In thinking this place is larger than what we can see? Yes. Come. Fawke is waiting."

"You could have called me."

"Need to keep moving or die. We're in the dining room when you're free." He limped back out.

Eb had lived in the underground compound his whole life, yet there was still much to be discovered it seemed. He'd been alone for so long, content to tend his gardens and keep the place running he obviously hadn't felt the need to look further. Me, on the other hand, suffered from a strong case of curiosity.

When Lars arrived, I headed to the dining room. The only room in the compound with enough room to spread anything out on a table. It had become not only a place to eat, but a meeting place.

Fawke glanced up and smiled. "Good morning."

"Good morning. Good news, too."

"Hopefully." He moved over so I could stand next to him at the table. "This is where we've been living." He circled an area with his finger. "The doors leading outside. But here is another door. One we've not discovered."

"It looks as if there is a lower level."

He nodded. "Maybe more than one. If we can find this, we'd have room to house a lot more people."

I glanced up. "You think more will come?"

"Yes. Mom said there's a lot of unrest in Soriah. Food shortages, water and power rationing. If her group could get out, then so can others."

Which would draw the Malignants back from wherever they'd been hiding. No one had seen one on camera in weeks. Common theory was that they'd gone to the mountain to avoid the army. But, if the city started to fill with people, would that draw them back?

"We need more room for gardens," Eb said. "We're running out of meat. Why not have someone find a way to catch those birds outside? These are the things we need to think about if our numbers keep growing."

By meat, he meant rats, something I did my best not to think about when meat was on the menu. "I'll get someone thinking about it. Will the pumps work for more gardens?" Right now, rainwater was captured in a huge basin, then filtered to rid it of the poison that kept humans and Malignants inside during the rain.

"Something else to deal with." Eb lowered himself into a chair. "I can't remember how my father did all this, but their numbers had to have been as big as ours."

"I can't believe you haven't explored." I sat across from him, my mind spinning with the preparations we'd need if Fawke's assumption was correct.

"It took all my energy to keep up with what I have. You're the leader. This falls on your shoulders now. I'm an old man nearing the end of my days."

Which was another thing to consider. Where would we put people when they died? So far, we'd lost them to the army or Malignants, but people in the compound would die. Death was inevitable. I needed to make a list, in order of priority, of what needed doing. First, find the door that led down.

I studied the blueprint deeper, flipping it to look at the next one. "What if each of these pages are a separate floor? There's five, if I'm correct, and a myriad of tunnels." A possible five stories that could provide solutions to the problems we faced. "Eb?"

"My father would have known. I didn't take over until he died. A lot of what I do, I had to learn."

"I want to go outside." I planted my hands flat on the table and pushed to my feet. "I'd like to study the entire area the amusement park had once stood on."

Fawke nodded. "Let's go."

After stopping by the infirmary to collect our weapons, Fawke and I stepped into the wasteland of a once prospering city. A city Soriah now wanted in order to expand.

"Area's clear," Lars said into my earpiece.

I stepped from behind the pile of debris we used to cover our entrance. Time had claimed the area, covering everything with a gray dust. Bombs, both recent and decades past, had finished what nature hadn't.

"How big do you think this park was?"

"Let's assume it spread to where the taller buildings started. I'd say acres."

"Then the compound is only a very small portion." I climbed on top of the debris to get a clearer look.

Weeds stretched for a mile in every direction. Smaller buildings, in varying degrees of decay, poked up from the weeds. There would have been many more rides than the Ferris Wheel that hid our compound. What had happened to them?

I jumped off the pile and moved slowly through the dried weeds. A flock of birds cawed overhead, disturbed by our presence. I swept my foot through the dust in search for what had once been there. There had to be evidence of other rides.

"Where did everything go?" I glanced at Fawke. "It's as if someone removed everything."

"Smaller bits would be buried under several feet of dirt. Parts would have been used for repairs in the compound. We could ask Eb. Is that what we're out here for?"

"Mostly to get an idea of how big the compound is. I can't imagine Eb's father and his people not using every bit of what was available."

"I agree. Jenkins might remember something. He lived here before his father led a group to the mountains."

True. I gazed to where the mountains rose in the distance. A place I'd loved until the army discovered the Rebel City. Even with the gray that covered everything, I preferred outside over the confines of underground. "Let's talk to him."

We returned to the compound and headed to the training room where Jenkins taught a few teenagers how to wield a sword. "Sure, I remember there being other things buried in the dirt out there. My father had some things dismantled to use the materials to build our home on the mountain. I don't remember any floors below this one, though. But, we left when I was small. You really think this place is much larger?"

"If the blueprints are correct, yes."

"Wow. A life changer." His eyes widened. "This place could hold more people than Rebel City ever could and go undetected."

"That's the plan." I turned to Fawke. "Let's find that door."

After another study of the blueprint, I followed Fawke to the room where Eb had stored supplies. All weapons and ammunition had been moved to the armory. Bolts of fabric and boxes of food packets still filled the space. A large shelving unit full of tools covered most of one wall. That's where the door should be. But why cover it up?

It took over an hour for us to clear the shelves and be able to move the unit. I stared at the door we'd uncovered. "Why hide it?"

"Maybe there's something behind it no one wanted found."

Dread filled me. Curiosity had me reaching for the door.

"Crynn to the control room." Lars's called over the intercom had me pulling back from the handle.

Fawke laughed. "Maybe we really aren't supposed to open that door."

"Oh, we're going to." I whirled and marched to the control room.

"We've got a big problem," Lars said the second we entered. "Take a look." He rolled his chair away from the monitors.

I stepped up.

My blood ran cold.

Marching from the gates of Soriah came soldiers numbering at least a hundred. Behind them came tanks and a large truck which most likely carried supplies. "Where did they get that many?"

Fawke peered over my shoulder. "Some of them aren't more than kids."

"I don't think The Wheel matters anymore. They're snatching young people from their homes and handing them guns." Which made our job a lot harder. I didn't think I could kill a kid, even if they pointed a gun at my head.

2

"We might get more to deflect," Fawke said.

"What we need are soldiers, not inexperienced kids." I paced the control room, once again regretting the spin of that cursed wheel that landed me in the burned-out city as a leader.

"We take what we can get and train them." Fawke put his hands on my shoulders, stopping me. "You got this, Crynn. *We* got this."

I gave into a moment of weakness and leaned into him. "I'm so glad I'm not doing this alone." The responsibility would crush me.

"What do we have here?" Lars pointed at the screen. "If you two are done cuddling, you might want to see this."

I stepped reluctantly from Fawke's arms and stared at the monitor. Five people darted from Soriah before the massive gates closed. Staying to the shadows, they skirted the army. Anne was right. More would flee the oppressiveness of President Cane's rule. "We have to go get them."

Before we could leave, the radio screen flickered to life. I stepped in front of it to block the view of the control room. "Hello, Sharon. It's been a while."

"Miss Dayholt." The woman's smile didn't reach her eyes. "I'm giving you a chance to surrender. The army is too strong for you to win this war you've started."

"President Cane started this war when he sent eighteen-year-olds here on a lie. He used kids to fight monsters so he could reclaim a city he destroyed."

"There is more here than you know, Miss Dayholt. The city was destroyed to clear it of monsters."

"Instead, it made them worse. They're breeding now. By sending more people here, you're only making the Malignants stronger. Giving them a buffet."

Shock flickered across her face. "Have a good day." The screen flickered off.

"Did they really think the Malignants would be that easy to eradicate?" I met Fawke's gaze.

He grinned. "At least they still believe you're a threat. Let's get to those refugees before the army spots them."

"Be careful out there. With the army so large, getting around unspotted won't be easy," Lars said. "Keep your ears open. I'll be your eyes the best I can."

Our boots thundered on the concrete floors as we raced for the exit. Outside, we waited for Lars's directions.

"Head toward Soriah, staying to the east to avoid the army. The refugees are heading toward a courtyard. They'll be trapped in there."

I knew where he was taking us. With Fawke on my heels, I sprinted in that direction. The entrance to the courtyard looked like an easy pass through. Once, it might have been. Now, the collapse of the buildings around it left anyone who entered with only the one way out.

A sound I hadn't heard in weeks chilled my blood. A Malignant shrieked. The marching army woke them from whatever slumber they'd been in, lured them from their hiding places. Did the monsters hibernate as we approached winter?

I pulled my sword and ran faster, racing up one block, cutting over, and up another. The Malignants wouldn't attack the hundred marching soldiers, but the small group of civilians was a perfect target. "Where are they, Lars?"

"Catching up to the smaller group. There's three Malignants. One looks like a juvenile."

"We can take them," Fawke said. "From now on, we take more than just us two. If they're active again, it's too dangerous to venture out with less than five fighters."

"Agree." I slowed as we neared the courtyard and sniffed. Now that the oil fires no longer burned, the stench of a Malignant was easy to detect. Not smelling one, I motioned Fawke forward and entered the courtyard.

Two men and three women huddled where a fallen building blocked their flight. I introduced myself and Fawke. "Do you have weapons?"

"Nothing but this iron bar I picked up," one of the men said.

"It's better than nothing. We're going to have to fight our way out of here. Don't come closer unless you have to." I stood back-to-back with Fawke and faced the entrance as the first Malignant raced in. They'd have to get past us to get to the unarmed people.

One of the women screamed, no doubt surprised that the monsters from scary stories actually existed. Two more Malignants followed the first, filling the air with their shrieks.

The creatures circled us, moving closer like the fighters Jenkins once pitted against each other to prove a person worthy enough to stay in Rebel City. I raised my sword.

The juvenile monster, eager and inexperienced, was eager to dispose of. I stabbed my sword into its chest and whirled to meet the attack of a larger one, dancing around it to stay out of reach of its claws.

It leaped forward.

I fell to one knee and jabbed upward, slicing its cut open and spilling foul blood and intestines across my arms. Fawke spun, decapitating the other one. We'd killed them with hardly a sound. If the woman's scream hadn't alerted the soldiers, we could make it back unseen.

"That was impressive," the man holding the bar said. "We've heard rumors of your group and prayed you actually existed."

I frowned. "You left Soriah on a rumor?" I didn't know if that was bravery or foolishness.

"We couldn't stay. I'd been accused of stealing food."

"Did you?"

He grinned. "Yes, my wife is pregnant. We needed that loaf of bread. If I went to prison, she'd be left alone. Things are bad in the white city. I'm Gerry."

"They aren't easy out here. Stay close and do exactly what I or Fawke tell you. No noise, no screaming. We can't take on more than a few of these things at once. Understand?"

Three heads nodded.

Fawke peered out the sagging gate of the courtyard, then waved us forward. I sent the others out first, taking up the rear in case of an attack from behind. Where we'd made haste getting to the newcomers, we now moved at a snail's pace in hopes of remaining undetected.

The thump-thump of an approaching helicopter sent us crouching under the tilted roof of an empty storefront. A second following the first had me guessing the flight of these five people hadn't gone undetected.

"We can't head straight back to the compound," I whispered. "Not until dark." I turned to the others. "Couldn't you have taken the secret way out? You were seen leaving."

"There's a secret way?" Gerry's brow wrinkled.

"Others have taken it. There's a tunnel." Which I would find someday and enter where others only wanted to escape.

"We saw an opportunity and took it."

"While putting us all in greater danger." How had they managed to make any plans at all while being this disorganized?

"Quiet." Fawke crawled forward and peered out.

He scooted back and held up three fingers then used two fingers to mimic walking on two legs. Soldiers. Scouts sent to find what the helicopters couldn't.

We moved as far back as we could and waited. My hand sweated around the hilt of my sword, a weapon I couldn't use in such a cramped space. My heart beat in my throat as the sound of approaching footsteps grew louder.

Three pairs of booted feet passed our hiding place.

In the distance rose the shriek of a Malignant.

One of the soldiers swore. "Can't believe we got the task of finding those people. Why not let those things get them and be done with it?"

"Because the new commander told us to. Don't complain or you'll find your head on a stake."

Their arguing faded as they moved away.

I raised a brow at Fawke who shook his head. Stay it was. I released my tight grip on my sword and tried to get comfortable on a ground littered with rocks and chunks of cement.

As we settled in, the newcomers dozing, I ran again through my mind all the work that waited at the compound. Then my mind turned to the newly arrived soldiers. Soldiers that carried supplies and weapons.

We'd infiltrated their camp before. Could we do it again? We needed the things they brought with them. Since some of the soldiers had joined our ranks, we had uniforms. Could that be our way in? Hide in plain sight?

Another shriek of a Malignant, closer this time, sent a trickle of sweat down my back. This place would be our coffin if they found us. I stared at the blood covering my arms and scooted closer to the entrance.

Fawke put out a hand to stop me.

"The smell." I showed him my exposed skin.

He nodded, his features grim, as I settled near the entrance in hopes of disguising the humans behind me. A Malignant might pick me out of the shadows, but smelling one of their own confused them. I grinned. This was how a person hid in plain sight. The uniforms might just do the trick.

As the gray day turned to an inky black, I crawled from our shelter. Finding the coast clear, I waved the others forward. "Lars?"

"Bout time you guys got up."

"What do you see?"

"Getting too dark. While you hid, soldiers scouted, Malignants hunted, and I got to see a couple of the soldiers meet their demise at the hands of those monsters. It's been quiet for about an hour now. You're clear all the way home."

Fawke again took the lead, weaving around debris until the Ferris Wheel showed us the way. Inside, I turned to the newcomers. "We'll get you fed and find rooms. Married couples get their own, but others have to share. You'll be trained to fight, except for the expectant mother. Jobs will be found for you. No one gets a free ride." I glanced at Gerry. "No stealing. We share what we have. There's no leaving this place. Only fighters led by myself or Fawke go out. Capture means certain death. Questions?"

"So, we're prisoners." Gerry crossed his arms.

"Not at all. We are in a war. That means rules. You're safe here." I met his glare with one of my own. "If you have a problem, we'll send you back out there to fend for yourself. You will not survive. The time is coming when our army meets theirs. Will you fight?"

He glanced at his wife, then gave a reluctant nod. "Yes."

"Then welcome to the new Rebel City." I led them to the dining room and put them in the capable hands of Bethany.

Before I ate, I wanted to get the blood off me. To conserve water, I washed only what was exposed. It hadn't rained in weeks, but Eb had said winter would bring lots of rain. That meant rubber suits when venturing out. One more thing that needed taken care of. The seamstresses would have to get busy sewing the suits that would protect those who headed out.

I scrubbed my face. The rain would also keep the soldiers in their camp. If we wore the suits at night, we might be able to sneak in and out without detection instead of the riskier donning of uniforms and marching in.

A lot of risks to weigh. Things I needed to discuss with Fawke.

I donned a pair of loose pants and shirt and handed my ragged fighting clothing to the women in laundry before returning to the dining room and a bowl of vegetable soup and bread. I tore the bread into chunks and dipped a piece into my bowl.

Fawke sat across from me, his fighting garb also replaced with clean clothes. I told him of my options for entering the camp.

"I like the idea of using the rain as cover." He folded his arms on the table. "I barely survived the whipping I received. I hate to think of you suffering the same."

I gave a sardonic laugh. "They wouldn't waste the time. My head would be on a stake and marched through the streets of Soriah as an example." I straightened. "We need those supplies. Entering the camp is the only way to get them."

"Capture leaves these people without a leader."

"Jenkins can lead if I fall." I dunked another piece of bread into my soup. "I'm just a figurehead, Fawke."

"You're far more than that. You're a beacon of hope in a world of darkness."

3

I stood and stared at the door Fawke and I had uncovered. Would opening it unleash Pandora's box? Someone had covered it up for a reason. I knew I should wait for Fawke, but my hand seemed to move on its own, pressing a long silver bar.

Not having been opened for a very long time, the door wouldn't budge. I leaned against it and pushed. It opened with the shrieking of metal on metal. I stopped and listened to see whether anyone would come running to tell me to stop. Namely Fawke who would be upset I didn't wait for him.

Knowing he still slept and I'd woken from a dream of seeing him hanging from the pole in the army, his back shredded by a whip, I decided to investigate on my own. I flipped on my head lamp.

A tunnel stretched out before me. The floor dirt, the walls a maze of steel bars and concrete. Overhead ran electrical cords and pipes. I glanced at my feet where decades of dirt lay untouched.

I stepped forward. A plume of gray dust swirled

around me. I waited to see whether the dank, musty air was poisoned. When my body didn't react in an adverse way, I took another step.

"What are you doing?"

I gasped and whirled, reaching for my sword, and stared into the stony face of Fawke. "I didn't want to wake you."

"Uh huh. What if you would have opened that door to a horde of Malignants?" He crossed his arms.

"Then I would've regretted it."

"And let them into the compound after they ripped you to shreds." He reached up and turned on his head lamp. "Let's do this, but at the first niggling of something being wrong, we return and come back with a larger group."

"What are you expecting to find? I don't think a human has walked these tunnels in a very long time."

A rat scurried along the wall to my left. "Look, more food." I grinned, trying to joke him out of his foul mood.

It didn't work. Instead, he motioned me forward and pulled the door almost closed behind us. "I thought we were going to prepare to hit the army camp tonight."

"We'll still have time. It's early." The dirt floor muffled our footsteps as we walked.

The air held a chill that I didn't think had anything to do with the coming winter. This far underground probably kept it this temperature all year.

We stopped when we came to a T-junction. I glanced at Fawke to see which way he wanted to go.

"Stay to the right. We won't get lost that way."

I nodded and turned right. The tunnel continued without any sign of a door. My stomach growled reminding me I'd skipped breakfast.

Fawke pulled a protein bar from his pocket. "Grabbed these when I didn't see you in the dining room."

"You always think of everything. Thanks." I tore open the package. Hissing overhead made me freeze, the bar halfway to my mouth.

Fawke stared at the pipes above us. "I can't tell which way the air is moving. Toward our compound or somewhere else."

The hair on my arms stood at attention. Goosebumps pimpled my skin. "What if we aren't alone underground? Some of those who left with Jenkins's group all those years ago could have split off and formed their own community."

"It's possible, but we haven't seen any signs of other life out here since finding Rebel City or the soldiers."

"Maybe they never go up." I ate the bar quickly and unsheathed my sword, not wanting to take any chances of coming up on an unfriendly. I suddenly regretted leaving the door partially open to allow us an easy entry back into the compound and prayed nothing would sneak past us and into our home.

"That's assuming we aren't alone." He put a finger to his lips and moved forward.

My nose wrinkled at a foul order. I recognized the stench and put a hand on Fawke's back to get his attention. "Malignant."

We continued at a slower pace. The odor grew stronger. At another turn in the tunnel, Fawke held up a closed fist and peered around the corner. He jerked back and plastered his back against the wall.

I peeked around him. Lots of Malignants, too many to count quickly, slept in a large space, clearly hibernating. Time to leave before we woke them.

We headed back the way we'd come, keeping the wall to our left. We'd have to come back with a group large enough to clear out the creatures before we could explore further.

I glanced back as we headed down the first tunnel. A man stood at the far end. I blinked and he was gone. I waved it away as my imagination and continued after Fawke.

The hissing in the pipes had stopped. If Fawke hadn't heard it too, I'd think I'd imagined the sound. What if there were other survivors? We could grow our numbers against Soriah.

Fawke stopped so suddenly, I ran into him. "I thought I closed that door more than that."

I stared at a door that now stood wide open. "You did."

We raced for the door, skidding to a halt at the sight of Ezra, sword dripping with black blood, standing over a dead Malignant. "What in the hell have the two of you stirred up now?" He glared.

"There's a whole lot more where this one came from," I said. "Get someone to drag that thing outside and meet us in the dining room." I slammed the door closed and engaged the lock. I shuddered at what could have been a fatal mistake. "Gather up the rest of our core group and find Eb and Jenkins."

As Fawke and I headed in that direction, I told him of thinking I saw someone.

"A lone man in a tunnel full of hibernating Malignants? Doesn't sound possible. One person would not survive."

"We seriously need to explore that whole network."

"It'll take a while, but I agree. Let's deal with the first problem. Clearing the tunnels."

"Are we setting aside the army camp?"

"No. We need whatever supplies we can get."

In the dining room, a young girl brought us bowls of watery gruel. As we ate, the others slowly trickled in to join us.

"I got a couple of the younger men to drag the carcass out. Told them not to let anyone see them. We don't need to start a panic." Ezra plopped into a chair across from us. "I went looking for you two to start our meeting about our plans for tonight and ran across that thing sniffing around. You can imagine my surprise…and fear. Ready to tell us what's going on?"

Eb slowly lowered into a chair. His brow wrinkled as he glanced at me. "What's happened?"

"We found a door behind some shelves in the supply room," I said. "Fawke and I opened it today—"

"Letting in a Malignant." Ezra glared.

I cut him a sharp glance. "There's a series of tunnels, pipes, and electrical wires. We also found a large group of hibernating Malignants. I thought I spotted a man, but can't say so with any certainty."

Eyes widened and mouths dropped open as I talked. "We still plan on hitting the army camp tonight, if it's raining, but we need to clear out the tunnels and finish exploring. It looks quite expansive."

"If they got in here…" Kira's words trailed off. It wasn't hard to finish her sentence.

"You think there are others?" Gage asked. "People, I mean."

"Eb?" I tilted my head. "Did you not know about this?"

He shook his head. "I only know what my father told me. Those tunnels don't show up on the blueprints, and I didn't have those until recently. I had too much to do keeping this place running without checking out things I didn't know about."

"Is it possible there are others?"

He shrugged. "I guess so. I mean, why not? That first group, the one my father belonged to, was large."

"Until we discover otherwise, we have to believe any others are not friendly." Fawke exhaled heavily.

Jenkins rushed into the room. "Sorry I'm late. Two of our younger men got into a fight during training when one hit the other a bit too hard. What'd I miss?"

"Did everyone that left this place go with your father's group?" I asked.

"I don't know. I was just a kid. Why?"

Fawke quickly filled him in.

"Wow. This could really shake things up. We need to get a camera in those tunnels."

"Yes." I nodded. "After we deem it's safe to send in workers. Also, if something should happen to me, Fawke is in charge. Then Ezra. If Ezra falls, it'll be up to you to lead these people."

His brows rose. "You plan on dying any time soon?"

"No, but the danger is escalating. The target on my back is growing. It's best to have plans made. Tomorrow, we hit the tunnels. Let's talk about what we're doing the first night it rains. Kira, how are the women doing on the rubber suits?"

"Ten ready to go. They'll keep sewing as long as they have the material they need."

"Medical supplies?"

"A priority when we hit the camp. Same with food."

"I don't need to tell you that weapons and ammo are always a priority," Dante said.

"We'll split into two groups," Fawke said. "One to hit the medical tent, the other the armory. It will need to be a quick in and out. We aren't going to create a distraction that will give away the fact we're there. Dispose of anyone between you and your goal. Got it?"

Heads nodded.

"It'll be this group that goes, plus Jolt and Samson. I'm not taking any inexperienced fighters. If you fall, you may be left behind."

"No." I shook my head.

"Crynn, we can't lose a group over one. If you fall, and your group can get out safely with you, then so be it."

"I agree with Fawke," Ezra said. "We can't jeopardize the entire mission over one person. So, no one fall, okay?" He grinned.

"It isn't funny." I scowled.

"Look, little girl. We know the risks. We also

know it's something we have to do. Might as well lighten up." He stood and rubbed his hands together. "It's early. Who's ready to kill some sleeping monsters?"

Everyone was on board. I glanced at Jenkins. "This is a good time for your best students to get in some practice."

"I've got five promising ones. Jerome is one of them."

"He's too young."

"The boy is champing at the bit to fight. He may only be thirteen, but he's one of the best with a sword. If you'd work with him, he might someday be as good as you and Fawke."

"Make sure he's wearing armor. We meet in the supply room in twenty minutes." I didn't like the idea, but I couldn't protect the boy forever. He might as well gain experience before the real battle looming on the horizon.

As we headed for the armory, Jerome fell into step beside me as if he belonged there. His eyes wide in a dark face belied his bravado. He might be eager, but at least he was scared. Fear would keep him from making a costly mistake.

"I heard you're good with a sword." I smiled.

"I am." His chest swelled.

"You'll be killing something alive. Can you do that?"

"If it's trying to kill me, then yes."

"Have you ever seen a Malignant?"

He swallowed audibly. "On the way here. It attacked the man right next to me. I ran."

"Good. You might have to run again. If I tell you

to, no arguing. A good soldier follows orders. Now pick out a sword. Test the weight of it in your hands. Swipe and lunge without hitting one of us."

He studied the weapons hanging on the wall and chose one with a serpent carved into the blade. "Strike like a snake, right?"

"How do you know about snakes?"

"I read about them." He stepped to the side and practiced, before allowing himself to be suited up.

I met Fawke's amused gaze.

"I'll watch out for him," he said. "I can watch him and you both."

I smiled, knowing he would always have my back.

4

Fifteen against how many Malignants? Now that we'd opened that door, we had no choice but to dispose of them. "Jenkins, have fighters at this door in case they get past us. We cannot let them in with the general population."

He nodded, his face grim. "I'll have them and every door between here and the others closed. They won't get in."

Fawke pushed the bar to open the door and glanced over his shoulder. "Not how I thought we'd spend your birthday."

"My birthday?" I scrunched my forehead in thought. Had I really been gone from Soriah for a year? A year since I'd spun that cursed wheel.

"Your mother told me." He grinned. "We'll celebrate later or maybe you think destroying a nest of Malignants a sufficient gift."

"It'll do." I laughed.

After a chorus of happy birthdays, we turned on our headlamps and stepped into the tunnels. Fawke warned everyone to stay together. "We don't know how long the tunnel is or how many branches. We don't need anyone getting lost."

The new fighters, faces paled, nodded. Jerome walked so close on Fawke's heels that he had to be told to stop stepping on the back of Fawke's boots.

"Do you want to go back?" I asked him.

He shook his head and fell into step beside me. "I need the experience."

"True, but if you aren't ready…"

"I am." He squared his shoulders.

I glanced down the tunnel where I'd thought I'd seen someone. No one stood there. No sign anyone had stirred up the dust. Still, I couldn't shake off the idea that someone *had* been there.

The reek of Malignants signaled we were almost there.

"We stand back-to-back once inside," Fawke said, his voice barely above a whisper. "Do not break rank. They will shriek and attack the second their eyes open. Do not panic. Panicking will get you killed. Do not run. They will chase you." He looked from one new fighter to the next. "If you can't do this, head back now. Move in quietly. We'll kill as many while they sleep as we can."

Thankfully, no one left. We needed each and every one of them. I only hoped we brought enough fighters.

Fawke eliminated a large male near the entrance. Dante stepped in next and sent a plume of fire from a flame thrower into several nests, swinging the weapon back and forth. While effectively wiping out a number of the monsters, it also woke the ones he didn't kill. Dante fired again as they swarmed us until the weapon in his hands lost its charge. He dropped it and took up his sword.

We formed our circle, swords raised. The odor of singed flesh mixed with the stench of multiple Malignants gagged me. I swallowed against the rising bile and tried breathing through my mouth.

The heat from so many bodies raised the temperature in the room we'd entered. Perspiration, whether from the temp or nerves, trickled between my shoulder blades. My palms sweated. Praying I didn't lose my grip, I jabbed my sword forward, piercing the chest of a Malignant.

Jerome stabbed and slashed, light on his feet. The boy might have been scared, but in the face of danger he'd shoved that emotion aside and fought like a warrior, even letting out a yell each time he attacked, stepping a few feet from the fighting circle.

"Don't lose focus!" The command left me in the form of a growl.

He moved back to my side. Fawke fought next to him while the others protected our rear.

One of the new fighters screamed and fell under the onslaught of two Malignants. Ezra removed the head of one, kicking the other off the man, then disposing of the creature. He hauled the man to his feet and out the door of the room. "Try to get to the infirmary."

An infant monster bit at my boot. I pierced it through the back of its head and tossed it away from me. Its mother attacked with a shriek that vibrated my eardrums.

I dropped to one knee, slashing upward, impaling her. I yanked my weapon free and shoved her to the side. How many were there?

Gage screamed and fell to her knees. Dante stepped in front of her and whirled, preventing the Malignant that had bit her from attacking again.

"Can you fight?" I asked.

"Yes," she said. "For a bit more."

"When you can't go on, head back." Thank the Supreme Being we still had medicine left to prevent a bite from killing. But, we'd need more, reinforcing the fact we had to infiltrate the army camp.

"Crynn!" Jerome fell backward as a Malignant leaped on him.

I lunged forward, driving my sword into its back before kicking him away from the boy. "You bit?"

"No." He got to his feet and picked up his sword.

The fighting became a free for all. Our fighting circle broke up as the monsters crowded in. I shoved Jerome against a wall. "Keep your back protected." I took up a stance next to him as others also chose to use the wall to protect their back.

My sword grew heavy, my arms weak. By the time we'd disposed of the last Malignant, we had two more injured and a new fighter dead.

"Help the injured," Fawke said. "Bring the dead man. We won't leave him behind to be food for any Malignants still roaming these tunnels." He glanced at me. "You okay?"

"Yes, but you're bleeding."

"I'll get to the infirmary. It's not from a Malignant. Got too close to someone else's sword."

"Which means you have Malignant blood in that cut."

His mouth quirked. "How do you like your

birthday so far?"

"Still standing." I smiled. "Let's get our people home." I clapped Jerome on the shoulder. "You did good."

"I've never been so tired in my life. I feel sick." He bent over and lost his breakfast.

"A hot shower will do wonders."

"I reacted the same way after my first kill," Fawke said.

He led us back to the storage room, then led the wounded to the infirmary. I headed for the showers.

I dropped my bloody clothes on the floor and stepped under the shower. As I ran the soap over my arms and legs, I made sure I wasn't scratched or bit. Not finding any wounds, I finished and donned a pair of simple cotton pants and shirt, my everyday clothes while in the compound.

How many more rooms full of monsters did the tunnels hold? I wasn't naïve enough to think there'd only been the one. With all the rats roaming around, the beasts had food. Is that why we didn't see as many in the city? Had they gone underground? If so, how did they get in? There had to be a second entrance.

I headed to the infirmary. The man Ezra had tossed from the fight lay sweating on a bed. Gage lay in another one the flush of a fever on her face. Fawke, sporting a fresh bandage, sat in a chair while Kira gave him a shot.

"I don't think we'll lose any of the wounded," she said, "but we're running low on the anti-venom."

"All we need is a night of rain." I stood over Gage. "You'll be alright."

"I know, but there isn't an inch of me that doesn't burn like fire. Sorry I won't be able to go to the camp with you."

"If it doesn't rain for a few days, you can." I smiled and moved to Fawke. "I'm headed to the dining room. Coming?"

When Kira stepped back, he stood. "Right behind you."

A singing of Happy Birthday greeted me as soon as I entered the room. Mom walked toward me, a cake in her hand.

I couldn't remember the last time I'd had a birthday cake. Tears welled in my eyes. "How did you manage this?"

"Eb was gracious enough to let me have some precious flour. Happy Birthday, sweetheart." She kissed my cheek. "I have a gift for you, too." She pulled a simple gold band hanging on a chain from her pocket. "This was your father's. I know he'd be so proud of you." She slipped it over my head.

"I can't remember a time you weren't wearing this." I touched the ring.

"It's yours now." She stepped back with a trembling smile. "Let's have some cake. You've had a busy morning."

Anne, Fawke's mother fussed over his injury. "Sit. I'll cut you a slice."

"I'm fine." He heaved a sigh.

"Let me take care of you. We've been apart for a long time." She limped to a sideboard and grabbed four plates. When she returned, she handed us each one, then cut four slices.

I waved Jerome over. "Join us. You deserve

something sweet."

"Really?" His teeth flashed. "It's been forever!"

I introduced him and bragged about what a good fighter he'd been. Both mothers turned their affections on the boy. He beamed under their attention.

"Now, they have someone else to mother," I told Fawke.

"Thank goodness." He forked some cake into his mouth. "I'm sorry I don't have a gift for you. I didn't know until this morning."

"Having you alive is gift enough for me." I ducked my head to hide the flush of my face and dug into the cake. When I'd finished and regained my composure, I lifted my head. "Do you think there are more in the tunnels?"

"Yeah."

"We need to find their entrance."

"Which we could do, probably, if we knew how large the network of tunnels is. We'll have to keep exploring."

"That will take days."

"We've got the time."

True. Without the constant need to scour the city above us for the monsters, our days were empty. Since President Cane had sent the army, no more scouts or scavengers arrived for us to steal from. I spent an hour a day sparring with those learning to fight, but that was a small portion. Searching the tunnels gave us something to do.

"I like the idea of another way out of here in case of trouble." I pushed my plate away. "If we can disguise the door in the supply room, it will give the women and children a place to escape in case the army ever gets in."

"That's a great idea. I'll talk to Eb about replacing the door with a secret panel."

"When is your birthday?"

"I'll be twenty-nine in two weeks. A year ago, I was preparing to return to Soriah."

"Until I messed that up." I remembered how angry he'd been with me for wanting to go to the mountain. I didn't blame him. Ten years hunting Malignants would have seemed like a lifetime.

"You opening my eyes was the best thing that could've happened. What I'd wanted most of all was to see my mother again. Now, she's here. There's nothing for me in Soriah. Never was from the moment you landed." He took my hand and pulled me closer. "Happy Birthday."

I closed my eyes as he leaned over to kiss me.

5

"I found them!" Eb dropped a pile of ledgers on the table in front of me. "Been looking my whole life."

"What are they?" I glanced up from my breakfast of powdered eggs. At least I thought that's what I ate.

"My father's journals." He sat across from me. "Every night, I'd watch as he wrote in them, noting everything that had happened that day. What worked, what didn't. I bet the truth of what happened to this world is in those pages."

"A priceless find." I grinned. These books held information I doubted we'd ever know without them. At least I hoped they did. "Where did you find them?"

"In the ceiling. Well, the man fixing a burned-out lightbulb found them, but here they are." He looked pleased with himself, his wrinkled face more so with the huge smile gracing his face. "Since my eyes aren't what they once were, I want you to read them. I have my ledgers in my room if you want them."

"When I finish with these." I'd love to know what

had gone on here before we arrived. "I doubt you have much since you were alone."

"Mostly gardening and jotting down when something broke." He pushed to his feet, his hands shaking. "I've been spending a lot of time with Jenkins and Lloyd, passing on what I know of this place. Someday, someone else will have to carry on with what I do."

"You'll outlive us all."

"There's a chance with the dangers you fighters embrace." He turned and shuffled from the room, leaning heavily on his cane. He paused in the doorway and hunched over, then straightened and continued on his way.

The old man did seem to feel his years. I gathered up the ledgers and stashed them in my room before going in search of Kira.

I found her in the infirmary checking out our wounded. "Can you take a look at Eb? I think something is wrong with him."

"More than old age?"

"Maybe."

"If he hasn't had breakfast, I'll take him a plate."

Assured she'd look out for him, I returned to my room and opened the first ledger. I grabbed a pencil and a pad of paper to jot down notes of interest.

Almost a hundred people, men, women, and children, had left Soriah in that original group. Eb's father mentioned escaping through a hidden door, but didn't mention where the door could be found.

One year later, the bombs fell. No mention of who had fired them, but Eb Senior had suspected Soriah to be the culprit. Why?

I sat back in my chair. Why destroy an entire city that could have housed people? There were no Malignants before the bombs. Who had Soriah wanted to eradicate? If they had been the ones to fire. Maybe another country…a war. That's what we'd been taught in school. Our teachers had told us no one but those in Soriah were left in the world.

Now that I was an adult, I questioned that. Eb's father had brought people out. Some had gone on to the mountain. How had they traveled safely through a city where the very air they breathed was poison? Had some of them turned into the monsters that roamed the area?

I turned my attention back to the open ledger in search of answers, scrolling past the mundane day-to-day notations. Eb's father had thought of everything when he and the others had fled Soriah, bringing with them seeds and tools. Everything they needed to survive and build. He'd known the amusement park had a space big enough to house them. Suspected there might be more but hadn't found evidence of other underground compounds, although he did know about the subways full of monsters. He'd taken a group wearing gas masks out of the compound.

When they'd run into the monsters, they'd returned here never to venture out again. But someone had. Jenkins's group.

I flipped the pages, wanting to know why the group had left. Ah. A falling out over leadership. They'd donned the gasmasks and left. Another reason for Eb's father to never leave. They couldn't, not safely anyway.

"What are you doing?"

I jumped at Fawke's question. "Eb's father's journals."

"That's a great find." He stepped into the room and sat on my bed.

"He suspected Soriah dropped the bombs, here and overseas, wanting to eradicate everyone not living in the white city. The bombs fell one year after his group fled. Fawke, he believed there were other compounds. There might very well be other people out there. If we find them, we might have an army large enough to fight."

"I've been here for eleven years and not seen any sign of other people except for those dropped from a plane or sent to scavenge the city. Not until the army and those in Rebel City."

"Doesn't mean they aren't there."

He shrugged. "You're right. Let's assume there are more. How do we find them? They obviously don't want found. I've been to every corner of this burned-out place."

"I'll keep reading. Are you ready to explore the tunnels more?"

"Yep." He got to his feet. "Hopefully, we'll get rain tonight. The winter rains are late this year."

I marked my place in the ledger and stood. "Unfortunately, the cold isn't late." I grabbed my coat and followed Fawke to the armory.

Once we had our weapons, we headed into the tunnels, making sure to close the door behind us. The sight of a man installing a camera startled me.

"Eb said you wanted these out here," he said.

"I do, but you shouldn't be alone. There might be

more Malignants. Get someone to watch your back. If you have enough, I want cameras at every T-junction."

"Only got two that work at this time."

"Better than nothing."

We passed the room of dead Malignants. I covered my nose with my hand to mask the odor of decay. "Really need to get some people in here to bury these things," I mumbled.

"Who do you want to punish?" Fawke arched a brow. "Foul job."

I agreed, but it still needed to be done. "I'll do it."

He groaned. "Which means I'll be here too."

I laughed, knowing he'd be digging right alongside me. "If we had prisoners, we could make them dig."

The air cleared a few yards past the room of death. The tunnel curved to the left. We passed other small rooms, but saw no sign of Malignants.

"Who do you think dug these tunnels?" I asked. "The same ones who built the compound?"

"Maybe they were thinking of expanding and never got around to it."

"The ones who did dig all this had to be here when Eb's father arrived."

"You might read about them in the journals."

A thud sounded around the next corner. Fawke held up a hand to stop me and put a finger to his lips.

We turned the corner. Nothing.

"Look," Fawke whispered. He pointed to an area where the dirt had been disturbed. "Looks like a scuffle." He glanced down the tunnel. "We aren't alone down here."

A chill ran through me that had nothing to do with the temperature. Malignant or human, where did they go? I hadn't heard the sound of running feet.

I ran my hands over the dirt wall, searching for a hidden door. Living things did not just disappear.

"Come on. Keep following the overhead pipes. They have to go somewhere." Fawke continued leading the way.

I followed, glancing back to the scuff marks in the dirt that didn't look like a Malignant had left them. I pulled my sword, feeling safer with the weapon in my hand.

The tunnel curved around again taking us back to the T-Junction where the second camera was being installed. "Did you see anyone?" I asked.

"Nope. Just the two of you." He climbed down from his ladder. "All set."

"Let's go back to where we saw the scuffed ground," I said.

As we went, I studied the dirt wall rising above us. There had to be something we were missing.

When we reached the spot, I studied the wall on both sides. Seeming to pick up on what I was looking for, Fawke did the same. He placed his hand over a rock that protruded from the wall. A soft click sounded, then a door in front of me slid open to reveal a dark room.

"Crynn, you need to get to the infirmary," Lars' voice came through my earpiece. "Now."

I sighed. We'd have to return later.

Fawke pressed the rock again, closing the door. "You were right. You've got good instincts."

We jogged back to the compound and returned

our weapons to the armory. I held firm that no weapons outside of training were to be carried and believed in leading by example.

"What's up?" I asked, entering the infirmary.

Kira turned, her expression grave. "It's Eb." She motioned to the bed. "He isn't well. I think it's his heart."

I rushed to the bed and gazed on the gray face of a dear man. His chest rose and fell in shuddering breaths. "Is he dying?"

"Do you know that he's ninety-five-years-old?"

"No." Tears blurred my vision.

"And, yes. I don't think he'll make it through the night. There's nothing I can do for him."

"He knew." I told her of his saying he'd been training Jenkins to take his place.

Fawke put a hand on my shoulder. "You stay with him. I'll do what needs doing today."

"Thank you." I pulled up a chair and took Eb's bony hand in mine.

I sat there all day, someone bringing me my meals when it was time. Those wounded in yesterday's fight had returned to their rooms, leaving me and Eb alone except for Kira who stayed close wrapping bandages in case Eb needed her.

"I wish you'd have gotten to read your father's journals," I said softly. "You would have felt so close to him. I'll read every page, soak in every bit of information, and carry on the work he started."

Eb squeezed my hand. His eyes fluttered open. "Good." He spoke on an exhale. "No...one...better."

"I thought you'd live forever old man." I blinked back the tears. "This place won't be the same without your knowledge."

"Be fine."

I didn't think so, but kept a smile on my face. "We found another room in the tunnels. We'll go back tomorrow to explore."

"Bet…lots."

"I think so, too. Why else would they have dug them? Your father doesn't strike me as a man who didn't start something that wouldn't be a benefit. Maybe he didn't dig the tunnels, but someone did. Maybe the people who built this place. That's a question that might never get answered." I blabbered on to fill the silence. "We're actually praying for rain. Can you believe that? Praying for poison rain so we can go to the army camp. I may have officially lost my mind."

The corner of his mouth quirked. His eyes drifted closed. "Love."

"I love you, too, Eb." I raised his hand to my lips. "Go in peace, my friend."

He took another breath, then a second…the third never came.

I choked back a sob and put my hand over his still heart.

6

Rather than the incinerator we usually used for bodies, we buried Eb in a corner of the garden he loved so much. I leaned into Fawke. "I'm going to miss that old man."

"I think everyone in this place will."

Jerome raced between two rows of corn. "Lars told me to tell you that it's raining. Coming down real good."

"We can wait." Fawke's arms tightened around me.

"No." I shook my head. "We're running low on medical supplies. Gather the group in the armory." Infiltrating the army camp would provide a welcome distraction of a place without Eb.

Leaving Fawke to get the others, I headed for the infirmary. I grabbed one of the rubber suits hanging on the wall and slid it on over my clothes before choosing my weapons. The sword, of course. Never left the compound with it. I slid a handgun into a holster on my hip, grabbed a box of ammo, and slung a laser rifle over my shoulder. Ancient weapons and new. Both kinds served a purpose.

By the time I'd finished, the others had arrived, along with Jerome. "Absolutely not."

"You said I did good."

"We aren't fighting Malignants this time. The army is far more dangerous. I won't have your head on a stake." I glanced at Fawke for help.

"Not this time." He clapped the boy on the back. "I'll take you out another day. I promise."

Jerome huffed and darted out of the room. I hated hurting his feelings, but a thirteen-year-old didn't belong on a raid no matter how skilled he was with a sword.

I faced the men who had fought the Malignants with us in the tunnels, plus a woman who replaced the one who had been killed. "You will follow mine and Fawke's orders completely. You new people will not enter the camp. You'll be on the outside of the fence watching our backs. Got it?"

Heads nodded.

"Good. We go as quiet as possible. Hoods in place, shields down. No skin left exposed." I lowered my shield and headed for the door that led outside.

Fawke stepped out first and climbed the pile of debris that hid the entrance. A few minutes later, he waved us forward. We swarmed over the pile like ants, blending into the landscape in our dark suits.

"You're clear for two blocks," Lars said through our earpieces. "I'll check after that. Nothing moving but you in this downpour."

Malignants couldn't take the rain any more than humans which worked in our favor. Unless Soriah had managed to outfit all their soldiers, the army would be in their tents. We could only pray the infirmary and the armor weren't heavily guarded on a night like this.

We slipped through the city like ghosts. At times the rain came down so hard visibility was reduced to a few feet in front of us. The cold seeped through my suit, numbing my fingers, making me wish for the gas fires that had burned consistently up to a few weeks ago.

"Hold up." Lars said. "Nevermind. Thought I saw something. The rain is obscuring the cameras."

"See any army activity?" Fawke asked.

"Not a thing. I doubt they expect an attack in this downpour. Oh, and that radio from Soriah keeps going off."

"Let it," I said. "Won't hurt to let Sharon wonder what's happened to me?"

The lights of the army camp glowed through the rain, guiding us. When we reached the fence, Dante stepped forward.

"Wait." Fawke reached out a hand to stop him, then picked up a rock. "Might be electrified." He tossed the rock. When nothing happened, he motioned Dante forward.

Dante clipped the chain link and rolled it back enough for us to squeeze through. I directed half to the armory and the rest with me and Fawke, leaving the new fighters to guard the opening.

Fawke led the way behind the tents. When we reached the infirmary, he cut through the canvas.

When no cry of alarm came, he slipped inside, me on his heels.

A doctor whirled, his eyes wide. "Thought you were those monsters," he whispered.

I tilted my head. "Are you alone?"

"Except for one soldier asleep. Take me with you, and you can take everything in this cupboard."

"You know who I am?"

"The rebels."

"We don't have protection for you from the rain."

"I've got a rubber sheet I'll wrap around me." Desperation laced his words. "I didn't join the army on my own. It was either this or prison. I refused to deliver a fatal injection to a woman I believed innocent of the crime against her. If I wasn't a doctor, they'd have killed me. Instead, they drafted me."

"You'll be coming with us at your own risk. I can't guarantee the sheet will be enough protection." I tossed him my pack. "Make it fast."

The doctor opened the cupboard and filled my pack before reaching for the one Fawke carried. Soon, both bulged with supplies. The man grabbed a duffel from under a desk and finished emptying the cupboard. He grabbed a folded rubber sheet from a nearby cot and wrapped it around him, leaving only his eyes exposed. Then, he grabbed a pair of goggles from a shelf. The man had been prepared for whenever we showed up.

"How did you know we were coming?" I inched toward the opening.

"I didn't. I planned on escaping tonight in the rain. Thankfully, I'll have company. Names Olof."

I glanced at Fawke, who nodded. If his instincts

didn't alert him that the man lied, then he could come. Another doctor would be welcomed at Rebel City, not to mention the wealth of information he could give us about Soriah and the army.

We slipped out of the tent and back through the cut gate. I watched Olof for any signs of distress. So far, his sheet seemed to be working.

Dante and the others joined us, loaded down with weapons and ammunition. A block away from the camp, we stopped.

"Who's the guy dressed like a ghost?" Dante asked.

"A doctor named Olof." I turned to Fawke. "That was too easy."

"Nobody will go in the rain," Olof said. "The last time it rained, a soldier thought it only a rumor about the poison. It wasn't a pretty death. Not even the new commander will go out. He will come looking for us once it dries up, though. Hope you've got a safe place."

"We do." I fished inside my suit for my scarf. "You'll have to go the rest of the way blindfolded."

"I understand. I could be a spy."

I wrapped the scarf around his head, over the goggles. I then tied a rope around his waist and around mine. Not ideal, but we couldn't expose any of his skin by having him hold onto us. "Sounds like the new commander is weak."

"He'll do what he has to."

"Is the army's sole purpose for being here to clear out the rebels?"

"Yes. You and those monsters. Once they have, they'll be tasked at rebuilding."

I had no intention of allowing them to complete the task. I turned and headed for home, helping Olof where I had to.

Inside, we headed for the showers to wash off the rain before removing our suits. Then, I led Olof to a room he'd share with our other doctor, Rupert. "Show him the ropes tomorrow, okay?"

Rupert nodded. "Glad to have you."

"I'm glad to be here." He plopped onto one of the beds and covered his face with his hands. "I'm more grateful than you know. Killing isn't for me."

"Glad to hear it." I delivered the medical supplies to the infirmary and headed for my own bed.

The bombs started the next morning. Olof hadn't been mistaken in saying his commander would come for us. I climbed out of bed, grabbed Eb's father's journals, and headed for the control room. "Random targets?"

"Yeah," Dayton said. "They don't seem to have a target. I thought they wanted to rebuild this place."

"They'll have to start from scratch." I widened my eyes as a bomb landed close to the compound, removing the top part of the Ferris Wheel. Far too close for comfort, but we were safe underground. "Keep me posted."

"Will do." He returned his attention back to the monitors.

I started to head to Eb's room, then changed direction for the dining room. Steps heavy, I entered and headed to the sideboard to see what breakfast had been prepared. Sliced tomatoes and bread.

"Who is in control of the garden now?" I spoke to no one in particular.

"Jenkins assigned the task to a couple of women," someone said. "They took care of the gardens on the mountain."

I nodded and headed for an empty table. I opened a journal and started to read. Seeds were cultivated from each crop to plant the next season. I jotted a note for more seeds to be set aside. If we continued to grow, we'd always need more food. What I really wanted was fresh meat that wasn't rat or black bird. But, I wouldn't send an army to the mountain. Not when it might be crawling with Malignants.

Doing my best to ignore the bombing, I kept reading. For years no one left Soriah after Eb's father. He mentioned the falling out with Jenkins's father quoting irreconcilable differences regarding population control. Eb's father had wanted to make sure the compound would always have enough room. The other man had wanted to create a new city. Well, he'd succeeded on that mountain until the army discovered them.

I put a slice of tomato on top of the bread and took a bite. What had the first people eaten until their garden grew? So many questions I'd like answers to in case we ever had to leave this place and start fresh.

"You look lost in thought." Fawke sat across from me.

"Wondering how we'd survive if we had to leave here."

"Why would we ever have to leave? I thought the goal was to get rid of President Cane and move back to Soriah."

"It is. But if we're ever discovered—"

"We won't be."

"How can you be so sure?"

He grinned and tapped his temple. "I just do." He sobered and reached for my hand. "Don't let the weight of this place settle on your shoulders. You have tons of help now. It's not just the seven of us hiding underground."

I laughed. "We are underground."

"But there's a lot more than seven of us. You're building an army, Crynn. I didn't think that possible."

I shrugged. "There are more people who want out of the white city than I thought. We'll continue to grow and run the risk of running out of space."

"That won't happen for a while. We'll keep searching the tunnels. I've got men dragging the Malignant bodies to the incinerator. That room can be made into smaller ones. We've got this. Don't worry so much."

"You're right. We're good down here. Eb's father thought of everything. I want fresh meat."

He arched a brow. "Not sure how that's going to happen. There's nothing out there. The black birds aren't bad."

"When was the last time one was caught in the net?" I cocked my head.

"It's been a while. Can't have the net out where the army can find it. I'll think of a better way. The birds are as big as chickens. Maybe we could capture a lot of them, keep them in cages in the tunnels, raise some, and gather eggs. What I wouldn't give for an egg." He got to his feet. "You keep reading. I'm going to draw up some plans, then go outside once the bombing stops."

"Let me know when you go. I'll want to survey the damage." The idea of fresh eggs in our future sounded amazing.

The tunnels were going to come in very handy.

54

7

"I found some drawings of traps in one of the books in the library and have some men building them." Fawke sat across from me the next morning. "It'll take a while, and a lot of birds, but we'll get the eggs. Ready to head back into the tunnels?"

Closing the journal, I nodded. "I'm especially interested in that room we found." The one it seemed someone had been hiding in.

"Still think there are others?" He arched a brow and grinned.

"Don't you think it's possible?"

"Of course, but it seems like we'd have seen evidence."

"We did. Scuffles in the dirt outside a hidden door." I stood and took my dirty dishes to the sideboard. "Let me lock these in my room and I'll meet you at the armory."

"Oh, and good news. We have our first baby in the infirmary nursery."

I smiled and went to my room, my steps light. A baby meant a successful community. I knew that they were being born on the mountain, but this was the first here. The future looked a bit brighter.

After putting the journals in a small chest that I could lock, I went to meet Fawke. I chose only a headlamp, earpiece, and my sword. If we ran across another group of hibernating Malignants, we'd return with others. This was strictly a scouting mission.

"I want to come." Jerome stood in the doorway, arms crossed, a determined look on his face.

"Shouldn't you be in school?" Fawke said, entering the room.

"Why do I need that stuff?"

"So you can read and figure when you need to build or fix something." He strapped on his sword.

"I already know how to fight. You can teach me how to build, and Dante can teach me how to fire the big weapons. That's all I need."

I bit my lip to keep from smiling and explained about the journals and how much they were teaching me. "If I couldn't read them, I wouldn't know much about this place. With Eb gone, it's up to us to keep the people safe. That means the young need an education."

"This is education." He would not be swayed.

"Fine, but I'm going to tell your teacher to give you double the homework."

"You're mean."

"You have no idea how mean she can be," Fawke said, laughing. "Get your sword and a headlamp."

He rushed to the wall and grabbed his weapon. "Will we have to fight today?"

"Probably not." I connected the headlamp around my head. "We're only trying to see where the tunnels lead. You'll be bored."

"No, I won't."

I smirked. We'd see how long he stayed happy when all we did was march down one tunnel after the other. "You do exactly as we say or we'll bring you right back here."

"Okay."

Fawke led the way, leaving me to close the door behind us. We clicked on our lamps and headed right at the first opportunity.

I glanced in the room where the Malignants had been, surprised to see it had been cleared of the bodies and nests. The room could now be converted into three apartments when the need rose.

Fawke pressed the slight mound on the wall and opened the secret door. He stepped inside, then called us in. "These generate electricity. Or they do with a power source."

Machines taller than me filled the room. No lights flickered or blinked.

"They aren't working."

Fawke studied one. "I think they run on solar power. Since there's been no sun in a long time, they've laid dormant."

"Electricity for what?"

"The compound under the amusement park is my guess." He wandered among the machines. "Eb's father had managed to get around no sun. Maybe his panels were stronger."

"The information might be in the journals." Curiosity aroused, I stared at the machines. With all the bombing, the solar panels outside would have been destroyed a long time ago.

"There's also an underground river somewhere," he continued. "Some of the power comes from there. Our showers, our drinking water. I haven't been able to find it, though." He put a hand on the dirt wall as if the river would be on the other side.

I glanced at the floor. A river close enough for us to use would have to be under us. "We could search outside the city, find the source."

"As long as we have water, we're good, but it would be nice to know where our water comes from in case it does stop." He turned and led us from the room. "Let's keep following the overhead pipes."

"You're right, this is boring." Jerome slouched. "How long are these tunnels anyway?"

I laughed and kept going. "That's what we're trying to find out."

"I think you're being followed," Lars said through my earpiece. "I think I caught a glimpse of someone run past the camera."

"Let us know if you see them again." I turned as Fawke headed back the way we'd came. I put a finger to my lips for Jerome to remain silent.

My heart pounded. We were about to prove my theory right.

Rounding the corner, I caught sight of a foot right before it disappeared around yet another corner. "There is someone out here." I increased my pace, despite Fawke's warning.

A man sprinted down a straight tunnel.

"Stop!" No longer worried about being quiet, I kept up the chase, the other two following. Our feet pounded the packed dirt.

Jerome passed me. I couldn't let him confront the

stranger alone. Fawke darted past. I was fast, but nowhere near their speed.

When I caught up with them, the man stood against the wall, Fawke's sword at his chest. "Where did you come from?"

"I'm not telling you anything." The man's voice was muffled by the gas mask he wore.

"How many others are there?" I asked, my chest heaving.

"I ought to be asking you that question. We've been down here for years. Are you the ones causing the bombing?"

"In a roundabout way. How long and how many?"

He pressed his lips together.

"What are you doing in these tunnels?" Fawke pressed his sword more firmly against the man's chest.

"Same as you. You the ones that killed that room full of monsters?"

Fawke gave a slow nod. "You'll be coming with us. Crynn, your scarf." He held out his free hand.

The man slapped the scarf from his hand. "You're not blindfolding me."

"Afraid so."

I removed his mask.

"You trying to kill me?"

"The air is no longer poisonous. Just the rain." I picked up the scarf and tied it tight around his head. He didn't fight me. Movement caused the sword in Fawke's hand to poke harder. After blindfolding him, I patted him down, surprised not to find a weapon.

The man's clothes had been patched so many times, it was hard to see where the original material started. I glanced at the thick boots on his feet, then back to his face. He didn't appear starved, so got food from somewhere.

"Let's take him back. We can question him there." I glanced at Jerome. "Still bored?"

"No way." His teeth flashed.

Fawke stepped back and pushed the man ahead of us.

He stumbled, but caught his footing. "You going to kill me?"

"That depends on you," I said. "We don't relish killing. But we won't allow you to leave."

"Ah, you found him." Lars sounded astonished. "Wasn't sure I'd really seen him."

"He's kind of feral." I laughed.

The man cursed. "My people will come for me."

"I doubt it. You aren't armed, so they most likely aren't either. Aren't you afraid of the monsters?"

"They're hibernating. I only roam the tunnels during the winter."

Fawke prodded him through the door Jenkins opened and down the hall to the one prison cell we had. There he removed the blindfold and locked the man behind bars. "Ready to start talking?"

"No."

"This will be your home, then. Your meals will be brought to you." He spun on one heel and marched from the room. Jerome glanced at me, then followed Fawke.

I sat on a stool and faced the cell. "You do realize it's only a matter of time before we find your people.

Somewhere, there's a door. That door will allow us into your camp. I doubt you live above ground. Not with the army presence."

"Army?" He frowned. "What are you talking about?"

"Soriah has sent an army to dispose of anyone not willing to pledge allegiance to them."

"We're just minding our own business."

"How long have you been down here?"

He shrugged. "All my life. I was born here."

"It doesn't look as if you're prospering. Tell me where your people are. Your group can join us. We have everything you need."

He shook his head. "No one knows we're even here. They'll leave us alone."

"Do you know where the underground river is?" Maybe he'd be less suspicious of me if I changed the subject.

"No. We just get water from the wall. A spigot."

"No filter?" The water had to be filtered, didn't it?

"You're asking questions I don't know the answers to. It's just the way it's always been." Agitated, he started pacing. "I tried the door that obviously leads here once. When I couldn't get it opened, I went back and told the others there was no sign of life. How wrong I was."

"We haven't been here long. For years one person survived down here. Now, we're a thriving community intent on bringing Soriah to its knees."

"I don't know who Soriah is."

I widened my eyes. Had he really never been out of the tunnels? "It's the reason you live the way you do. Surely somebody has mentioned the city they fled?"

He shook his head. "Maybe the elders know, but they haven't passed on the information. Are you going to kill me?"

"No. We'll take you up and release you to make your own way." The man would never survive, but we couldn't keep him locked up his entire life. "Or you can join us by telling us about the others." I put my hands on my thighs and pushed to my feet. "Let someone know when you're ready to talk."

I returned to my room and the journals. This time, instead of reading and taking notes, I sped through the pages looking for any mention of a river. Ah ha. Eb's father mentioned an underground river that flowed from the mountain, then underground.

I went in search of Fawke, finding him in the training room sparring. "I know where the river is."

"Here?"

I nodded. "Come on." I headed to the cavernous space where the jeeps were stored. At the far end, settled into the floor, was a steel door. "I believe it's under here."

"We haven't been able to open that."

"Find a way."

"You're stubborn when you sink your teeth into something. Do the journals mention where the river originates?"

"The mountain. We'll need to find it before the army does." I locked gazes with him. "If they find it, they may dam it. We have to protect this resource. Cutting off our water supply is a sure-fire way of getting us out of here."

"I agree." He dug in a crate and pulled out an iron bar. "Stand back."

It took several hard whacks before the lock broke off the door. Fawke grabbed the handle and pulled. The river rushed below us.

"I want this checked every day to make sure the flow doesn't slow down," I said. "Let's make plans to visit the mountain. I bet Jenkins knows exactly where the river starts to go underground."

"He has to stay. We can take Lloyd with us. He'd know."

Good. Two pressing matters resolved. Meat and eggs in our future and now the plan of protecting our water supply. Once those were complete, we could remain underground for as long as it took before taking the war to President Cane.

"Crynn?" Lars's voice came over the speaker. "Someone is knocking on the door leading to the tunnels."

8

I shot Fawke a startled look before tearing down the hall toward the armory. It might be time to always be armed now that we had others with us. Others we didn't know whether they were friend or foe. I grabbed my sword and sped for the tunnel door.

Fawke's thundering feet pounded in my ears. "Don't open that door, Crynn. We need to expect an attack. I've asked others to join us."

I paced in front of the door until Ezra and Dante joined us. Taking a deep breath, I nodded for Fawke to open the door, my palms sweaty on the hilt of my sword.

Shoving it open, he stepped back to my side.

One man, hunched with age, glared. "Where's my grandson, Sonny?"

"Behind bars until he starts talking," I said. "Who are you?"

"Name is Herb. I'm too old for games."

Fawke scooted a crate over for him to sit on. "You'll not get past this point without answering questions."

The old man slowly lowered himself to a sitting position. "We're peaceful. Stay to ourselves. There's no reason for you to hold him."

"How many of you are there?" I couldn't believe how tight-lipped these people were.

"Where's Eb?"

"He died. Answer my question?"

His face fell. "I'm sorry to hear that. He was my friend, once upon a time. Until my father took me away from this place and into the tunnels."

"Your grandson knows nothing of the above ground world."

He shook his head. "None of the younger ones do. We thought it best that way. Safer."

"Why did you leave?"

"My father wanted his own people to lead. Another group headed up. We doubt they made it."

"They did." I smiled. "In fact, they're back here with us."

His eyes widened. "But the air…"

"No longer toxic. Hasn't been for a very long time. The only thing to worry about up there now are Malignants, the army, and the rain." I pulled up another crate and sat to face him. "How many are in your group?"

"Fifty. We don't allow but a few babies a year."

I frowned. "How do you manage that?"

He squared his shoulders. "By forbidding it. We need population control. We have no marriages. Coupling is decided by the healthiest of the males and females."

Barbaric. "We're different here." I got to my feet. "Follow me. I'll take you to your grandson."

"Why not bring him to me? Save me the walk. It took a long time to get here."

"How long?"

"A day, but I move slower than most."

I glanced at Fawke. The tunnels must be huge. Could it stretch as far as Soriah? "Dante, bring his grandson, please." They didn't seem to be a threat to us. I turned my attention back to Herb. "How are you surviving?"

"We've water from the river, a garden, and rabbits and chickens."

"Rabbits? Chickens? How?"

"Brought with us all those years ago."

Excitement leaped in me. "Would you be willing to trade us some rabbits and chickens?"

"For what?" His eyes narrowed.

"What do you need?"

"Medical supplies?"

"You bring us the animals, and we'll bring out the supplies."

"Wise girl, aren't you?" He chuckled. "It's smart not to trust me, although you can. By morning, you'll have two female rabbits, one male. The same with chickens." It would take a while for them to produce enough to feed us, but the thought of fresh rabbit made my mouth water.

"Knock and the medical supplies will be brought out to you." I thrust out my hand. "Nice doing business with you. If you ever decide to join us, let us know. We're going to bring down Soriah."

"A lofty ambition." He pushed to his feet as Sonny rushed into the room. "Let's go home, boy."

"Before you go, do you know why Soriah

dropped the bombs?" I asked.

"To rid the world of everyone not residing behind their white walls. The group of people who found a way out was a slap in the face to Soriah." He shuffled through the door and into the tunnels, Sonny at his side.

Ezra closed and locked the door. "Never would have guessed there were people living under ground outside of this compound. This place has everything a person needs. Why leave?"

"Some men simply want power." Fawke motioned his head toward the hall. "Best go see what can be spared from the infirmary."

"Meet Fawke and I in the dining room in fifteen, please."

Kira sighed at our request. "All that hard work getting this stuff and you want to give it away."

"For fresh food, yes. Soriah will send more medical supplies." We'd take those, too. I'd told Lars to keep a look out for anyone leaving the white city.

"Alright. I'll get a box together." She didn't look happy about it. "I'll have the doctors help me."

"Thank you." Now to plan for our trip to the mountain.

Ezra waited at a table for us. "Where are we going? I'd rather be out there fighting, than in here playing maintenance man."

I laughed. "How does a trip to the mountain sound?" I explained our need to find the source of our water and prevent the army from damming the river.

"I don't advise taking all of our strongest fighters," he said. "Herb didn't seem violent, but he knows we have resources. What if he brings his people to take what's ours?"

"True. We'll take just the core group. We've got enough trained fighters now that can protect this place." We'll leave day after tomorrow. Let the others know." I felt safer surrounded by the group I'd met up with my first day. They'd become family to me.

"Uh, Crynn, control room." Lars interrupted our planning.

"What now?" I pushed to my feet and headed his way with Fawke.

"Take a look," he said when we entered. He rolled back his chair to give us room.

Three men in dark clothes, packs on their backs and pulling a wagon, tried slipping through the shadows. I smiled. Soriah didn't want to draw attention by sending a large number of soldiers this time. "Let's intercept. Call Gage and Dante to the armory." Kira would get her supplies replaced sooner than she'd thought.

"What if they're a decoy?" Lars asked. "To draw you into a trap."

"I don't think so. Soriah is building their army so they can attack without the danger of losing the fight. I don't intend on an outright attack on the army camp. Getting into Soriah and killing the president is our best bet at winning this thing." I glanced at Fawke who nodded, affirming my decision. "Right now, the camp is simply our place to get supplies. Like a market." I grinned.

"Don't get too cocky." Fawke clapped a hand on my shoulder. "They can get smarter and start expecting us."

"Of course." I marched to the armory wanting to leave immediately before the men passed our compound.

At the infirmary, we donned riot gear and armed ourselves with guns and swords. I slipped my earpiece into my ear. "Lars, keep an eye on our backs."

"Will do, boss. Right now, they're two blocks from here and moving slowly because of all the new debris the latest bombs caused."

Which would also make our journey tougher. "Let's go."

The four of us slipped out the back door and over the pile hiding our entrance. I stood and surveyed the area I hadn't set eyes on since the latest bombing. There were more piles of debris now than standing buildings except for the outskirts of town. The army knew we were hiding in the center. The good thing was…they'd never get their jeeps anywhere close to us now.

"If you go left three blocks, then turn right at the first street, you'll come up behind them," Lars said.

Fawke took the lead. We moved as fast as we could, which wasn't very with all the shattered bricks and iron bars. By the time we'd gone one block, sweat trickled down my back despite the cold. My breath fogged up the riot mask.

"Hold up. Two Malignants heading toward the three men and passing on the other side of the wall you're against." Lars's warning turned the perspiration to ice. "Okay, go, but you'd better hurry. Those things can climb over the debris a lot faster than you can."

"Come on." Fawke waved us forward, increasing his speed.

The three men might be able to hold off the Malignants, but if we could help them, save them even, they might join us rather than the army. Either way, we'd be taking the packs and wagon. It occurred to me that we'd become little more than scavengers in our quest to defeat Soriah.

"We'll never reach them in time," Dante said.

"Probably not," Fawke replied, "but we have to try."

Cries of alarm and the sound of gunfire proved Dante correct. I clambered over a short wall, taking a short cut, and landed in the middle of the fight. I pulled the handgun at my waist, shooting one Malignant in the head, then pulled my sword.

One of them fell under the onslaught of a fully grown Malignant landing on his back. The others fired wildly.

A bullet grazed my arm as I dove for cover, sending fire across my skin.

"Stop shooting or you'll hit her!" Fawke leaped over the wall, followed by Dante and Gage.

The four of us quickly disposed of the remaining two creatures before turning to face the survivors. These men weren't soldiers.

Fawke helped me to my feet while Dante and Gage trained their weapons on the men. Then, he faced them.

"Thank you," one of them said.

Fawke nodded. "We'll be taking those supplies. Sorry about your comrade. Who was he?"

"The new doctor. You must be the rebels we were warned about." He kept his own weapon trained on Fawke.

"The very ones who saved you from being torn apart. Lower your weapon or this will be where you die. You don't seem like a seasoned fighter and, I can assure you, we are."

"I see that." His hand trembled. "I can't give up these supplies or I'll be signing my death sentence."

"Either way, you're a goner." I took a step toward the wagon, pulling off my pack. "You going to shoot me again? You'll die."

"I didn't mean to shoot you."

"We thought you were more of those things," the other man said. He held up his hands, clearly not ready for a fight. "I'll come with you."

His partner frowned. "If you go with them, I have to."

"So? It's better than the army."

"How so?"

"Think of Mom and Dad. They're dead because of the very ones you think you're helping." His hands dropped. "They got sick and weren't important enough to help."

I widened my eyes. "Is Soriah getting short of supplies?"

He nodded. "Because we have to keep supplying the army with more. They're the only ones not considered expendable."

"None of our people are expendable." I glanced at Fawke. "What do you think?"

"I guess they can be trained to fight."

"Fight who?" the man asked.

"Soriah." I grinned. "We're going to bring President Cane to his knees or die trying."

The man holding the gun, lowered his weapon. "That's something I can get behind." He thrust out his hand. "Marshall, and this is my brother Bo. Can we get out of here, please?" He asked as a Malignant shrieked.

9

Back to the safety of underground, I headed to the infirmary with the supplies and to have my arm stitched. Kira's joy over the medical supplies was boundless. I smiled and sat down to let Rory, her assistant, tend to me.

"I thought the Malignants has mostly left the city," I said to Fawke who hovered in the doorway.

"I think the arrival of hundreds of soldiers has brought them back. It'll be hard for the army to keep them on this side of their fences if a large horde attacks."

"Not our problem." I averted my gaze at the harshness of my words. Had I become so fixated on stopping President Cane's barbaric way of running things that I'd lost any empathy for humanity?

The longer this so-called rebellion went on, the worse things would get for those still in the white city. It bothered me that their suffering was a direct result of my actions. Having the army fall would speed up the final confrontation and end their harsh life, allowing people the freedom to be what they wanted to be and not have their fate determined by a wheel or a dictator.

I glanced back at him. "I don't mean to be heartless, but we have other things to occupy our minds. The other group down here with us and securing our water source."

He ran a hand over his bald head. "I agree with you. The army has the weapons to defend themselves. They'd lose a lot, but that only helps us, doesn't it?" He turned and marched away.

Sighing, I stared at the floor, doing my best to ignore the pain of Rory's stitching. Fawke was the best fighter I knew, never hesitated to bring someone down if he had to, but his heart was bigger than mine.

Moses entered the infirmary, grease covering his hands. "Next time you're out scouting, we could use a new belt for one of the jeeps. I've done all I can."

"How things have changed since the minute I entered the hideout where you all were holed up."

He laughed. "I was surprised to see our new leader was a little girl."

"We don't have any plans on visiting the army camp anytime soon, but I'll keep my eyes out for a belt." Not that I had a clue what he was talking about. I'd let Fawke and Ezra know of Moses's request. "You sure there isn't one in the storeroom?"

"I'll look again, but didn't see what I needed. Eb's father had stocked this place well, but things do run out."

That's what drove me to find different ways of getting food and securing our water. "We're heading to the mountain tomorrow."

"I'll be ready." Without asking why, he left.

I'd never get used to people following my orders without question.

"All done. Keep it dry for a few days." Rory put tape on a clean bandage to hold it in place.

"Thank you." I stepped into the hall to see my mother rushing toward me.

"I heard you were shot."

"Just a graze, and it was an accident. I'm fine."

Her brow creased. "I hate that you're the leader. How I wish you were still that little girl with her nose in a book."

Her and me both. "Too late to turn back now."

She cupped my face. "I can't lose you again, Crynn."

"You won't. The group is leaving in the morning. We'll be gone at least a week." I spotted Fawke over her shoulder.

"Please be careful."

"I'll be surrounded by the best fighters we have." I gave her a hug and followed Fawke.

I caught up with him right before he entered the training room where a group of young men too old for school waited. I put my hand on his arm. "I'm sorry if I upset you."

"I'm just being soft. The army has to be dealt with. Having the Malignants take care of it for us would be the easiest way."

"It's not a nice thought for me either. The people here, though, take priority. It isn't like we can go up to the commander and say, oh, by the way, Malignants are returning to the city because of your presence."

"True." He smiled. "Want to help me train these

guys?"

I shook my head. "I need to rest the stitches, so I'll read some more in the journals. I'd like to see if I can find mention of Herb's group."

"I'll catch up to you at mealtime." He caressed my cheek, his eyes warming. "I could never be mad at you."

Leaning into his touch, I took comfort, then stepped back as the young men stared in our direction. "See you later."

I went to my room and opened the first journal. I found the mention of the others a little over halfway through. They'd left through the same door as Jenkins's group had, but Eb's father made mention of noises coming from outside the supply room door. Guessing it was them digging, he'd had the door barred in order to keep them from returning and taking supplies. In the interest of his own group, he'd written.

I could definitely relate. Every decision I made was for the people in the compound. I continued reading and taking notes until the bell chimed signaling our evening meal. I slipped a piece of paper between the pages to hold my place and joined my people in the dining room.

The next morning, I was wakened by a knock on my door. Groggy from lack of sleep due to my wounded arm, I shuffled to the door. I opened it to see Dayton. "Yeah?"

"The rabbits and chickens are outside. They're waiting for the medical supplies."

I blinked. "Couldn't you tell Kira?"

"Well, yeah, but I didn't know whether you

wanted to speak with them or not."

I sighed. "Wouldn't hurt to take a look."

After retrieving the supplies from the infirmary, I joined Dayton and Ezra by the door leading to the tunnels. I nodded for the door to be opened.

Ezra, one hand on the gun at his hip, opened the door. He grinned at catching me frowning. "You carry your sword everywhere."

I shrugged. Maybe it was a good idea to have a few of us carrying a weapon at all times. Accidents happened like it had when the Malignant got inside.

Sonny and five other men stood outside, making me wish I had grabbed my sword before leaving my room. I set the large box of supplies next to the rabbits and chickens, surprised at the amount. "This is more than we asked for."

"My grandfather felt generous. He really needs the medical supplies. People have died because we didn't have them."

"Do you have a doctor?"

"No, but we'll manage." He lifted the box and backed away. "Have a good life."

"You, too." I told Dayton and Ezra to bring the animals inside. The tension in my shoulders didn't leave until Sonny and the others rounded the corner out of sight.

I stared at the eight rabbits and same amount of chickens. "We'll need a large cage for the chickens. A coop, I think it's called. There might be a book in the library. I want the rabbits in separate cages and someone put in control of breeding. Build the cages in the garden room. The poop will be good fertilizer."

Ezra laughed. "How do you know this?"

"I read a lot as a child. Everything I could get my hands on, but I don't know how to build a chicken coop." I grinned. "We have meat, and we'll soon have eggs. This is a wonderful day."

"I'll get someone to take care of this and join the group for breakfast before we head out. I've already asked the kitchen staff to fill packs with food and water for our trip."

"Thank you for doing that." One less thing for me to do. I smiled at our bounty again before heading to my room to get out of the clothes I'd slept in and changed into what I'd be wearing on the trip. My very comfortable rags.

At breakfast, I joined those I'd be spending the next week or so with. The people who had my back so many times and the people I'd die for. Gage, Dante, Fawke, Moses, Ezra, and Kira. Later we'd been joined by Jolt, Lars, Dayton, and others who would remain behind to protect our home. Only the original seven would undertake this mission. Only the Supreme Being knew if we'd be successful.

"Whatever we take, we carry on our backs," I said. "I don't want to be slowed down by a wagon. If you can't carry it, it doesn't go." I eyed the seven packs that contained our food and water.

"I agree." Ezra nodded. "I don't want to be out there with the army so strong any longer than we have to."

The others nodded in agreement and dug into a double portion of oatmeal. Good. Starting off with a full belly would make our supplies last longer. I sat and started eating, my mind running over what I'd need from the armory. I already wore my sword. A handgun and a laser rifle were all I wanted.

Dante would want the flame thrower, but the big man could handle the weight. We'd steer clear of the army camp. I was in no mood for a fight. "Did anyone remember the rubber suits?" I glanced up from my meal.

"I did." Fawke held up a bag. "I've rigged this to attach to our backpacks."

"You always think of everything." I smiled.

"Don't want to have to hole up somewhere for days because of the rain."

"I want to come." Jerome approached our table, holding up a pack. "I've got my own rations, my sword, and a suit made to fit me."

I scratched my eyebrow and looked to Fawke for an answer. "Well?"

"He can come."

Joy radiated from the boy. "I'll be an asset. I promise."

"You'll follow orders to the letter." Our seven had become eight. I doubted he'd ever allow us to leave him behind after today. Jerome, although young, would be a fierce warrior someday. Maybe even take my place one day. "Let's get to the armory."

While the others chose their weapons, I headed to the gardens for another peek at our food source. Two men had gathered an array of wire and iron bars and were studying a book. One glanced up. "If you can bring back some wood, that would be helpful. Easier to work with than these bars."

"I'll see what I can do." Pleased they were working on the animals, I rejoined my group and grabbed my guns. I took a deep breath. "Ready?"

"Yeah." Dante nodded. "Beats staying underground all the time."

"I agree." I actually looked forward to the trip. Spending some time among the trees would be good for all of us.

"Let's do this." Fawke took a gun away from Jerome. "Sorry, but you've not been trained. Stick to your sword."

The boy opened his mouth to protest, then glanced at me and snapped it closed. "Right. Orders."

"A true soldier knows how to follow them," Fawke said. "I'll teach you at the first opportunity. Sometime when we won't attract attention." He marched from the room, leaving the rest of us to follow.

He opened our exit door and stepped out. Deeming the area safe, he waved us forward.

I followed into a cold so frigid, it took my breath away. The trip wouldn't be a pleasant one after all. In addition to the cold, I heard the rumble of jeep's tires.

10

I crawled and peered over the top. Two jeeps with massive tires drove over the debris as if it wasn't there. If seen, there would be no outrunning them. I slid back to the others. "We've got to stay low and make it to the outskirts of the city where there are still buildings to hide in. Lars, keep an eye on those jeeps."

"Will do."

Fawke darted across what had once been the parking lot of an amusement park and headed straight for the tallest structure still standing. With the jeeps still a block away, we had to hurry. Not an easy task with all the damage from the recent bombs.

The skyline seemed further than before as the army cleared out everything in the city's middle looking for our hideout. The mountain loomed even further, seeming impossible to reach in a few days.

After a few miles, we hunkered down behind a tangle of metal to catch our breath. The sound of the jeeps had faded away. Something far more sinister reached my ears. Something that sounded a lot like hammering.

"Is that what I think it is?" I asked.

"The sound of rebuilding?" Fawke nodded. "That's what I hear."

I'd thought we'd have more time before Soriah started rebuilding. Things must be worse in the white city than I'd thought. I peered through a gap in the metal toward the tallest building. "I can't see anything."

"We will." Fawke got to his feet. "Let's go. I have a feeling the jeeps are headed in the same direction we are. We have to stay ahead of them."

Despite his stating the obvious, I nodded. "Up, Jerome."

The boy popped to his feet as if he had all the energy in the world. "I don't know why you guys don't do this every day. It's exciting."

"We used to." Fawke tried ruffling his tight, wiry hair. "We kind of enjoy not having to now. Regular food and sleep is awesome."

"Boring, you mean."

I laughed. We'd see if he was as optimistic after we returned. I'd spent months out here and wanted nothing more than a permanent home. He'd tire of this life soon enough.

We ran again toward the building, stopping every half hour or so for five minutes before resuming. My lungs burned, my legs hurt, but after a while, the muscles remembered the life of a Stalker and grew stronger.

Shrieking to our right, sent us to the left. After a while, Fawke headed right again. He never seemed to tire. Neither did Dante or Jerome, but the rest of us was showing signs of growing weary.

"Almost there," Fawke said, glancing over his shoulder. "We'll find a place to stop for the night, taking turns at guard."

"How close to the rebuilding are you getting?"

"A building away, if possible. I want to see what is going on."

I disagreed. Getting too close raised the risk of being discovered. "Too close."

"It's not." He set his jaw.

I turned away, not wanting to have the others question his decision or undermine his authority. We'd agreed to co-lead, so co-lead we would. I'd not argue in front of the others.

A flock of blackbirds shot up from the weeds in the asphalt, cawing their displeasure. Fawke held up a hand for us to stop. When no shouts of alarm came from the birds' sudden flight, he continued, finally ducking into what could barely be considered a building.

Here, the sounds of work echoed. Hammering and something that shattered the air with a repetitive beating against asphalt. Fawke was right. While the work continued, they'd never be able to hear us. At night, we'd remain quiet. Wouldn't be hard as exhausted as most of us were.

"Let's go see what's going on," Fawke said, dropping his pack. "Ezra, would you lead the others in securing our camp?"

"Sure thing. Be careful out there." He reached out and grabbed the back of Jerome's shirt. "No way, buddy. You're staying here with us. Our job is important. Watch and learn. While the enemy makes noise, we can build our fortress. We need a strong man like yourself."

I smiled and followed Fawke. Jerome was in good hands. If Fawke and I fell, he'd lead the rest to secure our water source.

We ducked under a low beam, not worrying about noise, until we could see the soldiers through a space in the wall. Tools, wood, and crates were piled in front of where we hid. Two were labeled food, one ammo. I itched to confiscate them, but we had no way of transporting. Not until we returned from the mountain anyway.

Ten men scurried like rats, erecting walls and supporting a floor above their heads. They were definitely rebuilding. By doing one building at a time, it would take them years. Unless…Soriah planned on moving people out as space became available. But why? Malignants had returned. The civilians would be put in danger unless they discovered a way to keep the monsters out, which also meant those living inside couldn't leave the building.

When I expressed my thoughts to Fawke, he said, "I think they'll make each building a city in itself. I saw something in a book once. Water tanks and filtration system, a garden, all on the top floor of the building. A glass dome to keep the rain out."

"They can't possibly complete even one building in a short time."

"No, I wouldn't think so, but it appears they're trying. This could be a good thing, Crynn."

"How so?"

"The people of Soriah are unhappy. We'd have

hundreds of potential rebels in each building."

I didn't want to wait that long to bring down Soriah. This plan of theirs would take years.

The sound of rapid gunfire drew us away. We turned and peered into the street where a machine gun mowed down a small group of Malignants. Soriah would dispose of the creatures while rebuilding. It appeared they were no longer worried about us. They had more pressing concerns on their minds. Things must be very dire indeed. I'd contact Sharon when we returned and try to coerce information from her.

I turned back to the workers. One had placed his rifle near the spot we watched from. I slipped my hand through an opening and slowly pulled the weapon through.

"You've turned into a proper scavenger," Fawke said. "Let's return to the others."

"Can't let any opportunity go by."

The others had piled blocks in a haphazard way that concealed us and still looked random. Hot coals glowed under a pot as Kira stirred whatever our meal would contain. With the dust caused by the working soldiers, the odor from her cooking wouldn't be noticed.

Overhead, came the dripping of water. I glanced up, relieved to see the sudden rain couldn't penetrate the floor over our head. A slow drizzle at first that suddenly became a downpour.

I moved to the entrance. One of the workers had approached the jeep and now screamed and writhed in agony as the acid rain ate away at his skin. Not a way anyone should die. Even an enemy. I turned away from the horrible sight. We would be safe as long as the rain continued.

"Eat and get some rest." I sat, my back against my pack. "No one will come while it's raining."

"What about those things?" Jerome asked, his eyes wide.

"Not even them."

I accepted the bowl of gruel Kira offered, grateful for the simple, hot meal. When I'd finished, I leaned back and closed my eyes. We had no need of a guard, and since Fawke seemed to sleep with one eye open, he'd know the minute the rain stopped.

Night fell and the rain continued. We donned our rubber suits, slung our packs and weapons on our backs, and headed once more toward the mountain. I took the lead this time, Fawke taking up the rear. Without fear of discovering we moved as fast as possible along the buildings, using the meadow outside of town to allow us easy travel.

It didn't take long for the cold to seep through my suit. My teeth chattered. From their hunched shoulders, it wasn't hard to guess the others felt as miserable as I did. We couldn't chance a full blazing fire until we found cover away from the eyes of the army.

My mind kept drifting to the poor man who'd died in the rain. Were the soldiers really so dispensable that they couldn't be supplied with proper clothing? Maybe Soriah had sent too many to die out here. With winter in full force, we'd have more days of rain than not. Which, I hoped, would allow us one or two more visits to the camp before the rainy season ended.

"Soldiers on foot one block to your right," Lars said.

We slowed, staying low to use the tall dead grass as cover. Fawke put a finger to his lips and headed further into the field.

"What are they wearing?" I asked.

"Some kind of poncho."

So, Soriah did know about the danger the rain posed. The poor dead soldier had died by his own incompetence.

Deep in the field, the only sound came from the whisper of the wind through the grass and the patter of raindrops on my rubber suit. Relaxing and beautiful for something so deadly. I kept my eyes on the mountain where even more beauty resided. Someday, I'd live there permanently, never to go underground again until I was dead.

Fawke stopped suddenly. I peered around him to see the tall grass bowing against the wind. "Draw your weapons," he ordered. "Remain silent and do not move unless we're attacked. If Malignants are headed for us, they cannot smell you through the suit."

I drew Jerome close and held my sword at the ready. Malignants didn't venture into the rain. Their skin, paled from staying inside all the time except to hunt, was thin. No protection against the elements. Thus, they hibernated during the winter months. This was something else.

My heart beat in my throat as whatever stirred the grass ahead of us got closer. The rest of our group took their fighting stances, moving into position as silent as ghosts and setting their packs on the ground.

Whoever it was didn't seem to be in a hurry. I started to perspire despite the bitter cold. Maybe they'd go around us, never knowing we were there.

The rain sounded louder, the wind harsher as we stood stiller than the grass around us. Thunder and lightning rumbled and crashed overhead making hearing anything other than the storm impossible. If a squad of soldiers came our way, we were goners.

Frozen pellets of ice fell from the sky, pelting my suit with enough force to make me wince. It definitely wouldn't be Malignants coming our way.

Fawke frowned in my direction, mouthing, "What's taking so long?"

I shrugged, ducking as lightning struck close by. It wasn't safe out in the open. Adrenaline surged through me. I fought the urge to run for the nearest building.

The grass moved in another direction as whatever came toward us veered a bit to the left. We all shifted position, keeping our fronts to where the suspected danger would come.

"This is scary," Jerome whispered.

"You wanted to come. Shh."

"Nothing can hear me over the storm."

True, but why take chances. I narrowed my eyes and put a finger to my lips.

The grass parted.

Two poncho-wearing soldiers stepped out, eyes wide behind the goggles they wore.

We lifted our swords.

They lifted their hands.

11

The two people in front of us trembled, heads down. I motioned Dante and Moses forward. "Check them for weapons."

They were clean.

I frowned. "You're out here without a weapon?" Were they idiots?

"No time to grab one. The rain fell, and we ran. Can we put our hands down?" One of them said.

I nodded. "Who are you?"

"Deserting soldiers. I'm Yang, this is my…girlfriend Win."

"Why are you deserting?"

"I'm pregnant," Win said. "As a soldier, that means death. Physical relations are forbidden while on assignment."

Fawke cleared his throat. "Where did you think you'd go?"

"We hadn't gotten that far." Yang put his arm around the woman. "What are you doing out in this rain?"

"We're headed for the mountains," I said,

sheathing my sword. My breathing slowed, returning to normal. "You're welcome to come with us, but it isn't an easy journey. Otherwise, you're on your own." I wouldn't risk them being followed by soldiers anywhere close to the compound.

They whispered, heads together for a moment, then Yang nodded. "We'll come with you, please. We've heard about the rebels, hoped we wouldn't come across you as the commander said you kill on sight."

I grinned behind my mask. "Obviously, that isn't true. We're always picking up stragglers. It's their choice whether they want to be friend or foe."

From the widening of their eyes behind their shields, I didn't need to tell them what happened if they decided to be our foe. They gripped hands and stepped next to us.

By nightfall, we were far enough away from the army to chance camping inside one of the abandoned buildings still standing. Fawke entered first, checked for hibernating Malignants, then waved us in.

I was more than ready to get out of my rubber suit and stomped my feet as Dante built a fire. Once he had a good blaze going, we all stripped to our clothes. I narrowed my eyes at the sight of Win's very obvious baby bump. "How have you managed to hide your pregnancy?"

"I work in the kitchen. The apron did very well." She leaned against the wall, stretching her legs in front of her. "Yang is a sergeant."

I whipped to face him. "Can we trust you?"

"Of course. I'll do anything for Win and my child. Our only chance of survival is with you. Soriah would never allow us back."

"Why are the soldiers rebuilding? What's the plan?" I held my chilled hands over the fire.

"Soriah is bursting at the seams despite the trickle of people who find a way out. The elderly are living longer than they used to. They need this city, despite the danger of those things roaming the streets." He pulled Win close to his side.

"Have they stopped looking for us?"

"No, but you are not top priority right now. They aren't seeking you out, but have orders to kill on site. All but Crynn Dayholt."

I laughed. "That would be me."

"The president is scared of you, I think." He smiled. "No one has ever sparked a rebellion quite the same as you have. People are willing to die to escape the white city in hopes you'll find them. Soldiers are deserting every day, only to either be found by the army and killed or to die at the hands of the monsters."

"Yet, you were willing to take that chance."

"Yes."

Kira handed us all a military MRE. "Thankfully, these two did bring supplies even if they didn't manage to grab weapons. We'll be fine with extra mouths to feed."

"I'm more than happy to take over the meals," Win said. "I'm used to cooking for a lot."

I glanced at Yang. "What are your skills?"

"Weapon building and repair. You'll be quite happy with my new prototype." He reached for his food. "You'll find me very useful. My leaving is a great loss to the army."

"That must be the papers I found in your pack," Kira said. "I've replaced them. Couldn't make sense of the drawings."

"You wouldn't." He dug into his food as if he hadn't eaten in a while.

"How long have you been out here?" I sat cross-legged, balancing the meal on my lap.

"This is the second day. We hid all of the first. Then, when the rain started again, we left our shelter."

Smart man. Fawke had remained silent during our exchange. When he finished eating, he asked. "Can the two of you fight? Not that it's required for a mother."

"We're trained in gunfire, not swords," Yang said. "The commander calls swords primitive."

"They're useful against the Malignants when you don't want to alert any more of them close by." Fawke crossed his arms. "I don't want to give you a weapon. We don't know you or whether we can trust you. If we get into battle, then I'll give you a handgun." His gaze flicked to Win as if warning Yang that any treachery on his part would result in something unpleasant for Win. "Are you healthy enough for several days across rugged terrain?"

"Yes." She hitched her chin. "I'll keep up."

"If not, you'll have to hole up somewhere and hope you're still alive when we return. Get some sleep everyone. We leave in four hours." Fawke lay back against his pack and closed his eyes.

Fawke woke us in four hours. The storm had slowed to a drizzle. We donned our protective gear and headed back into the field, our goal looming ahead, a dark silhouette against a gray sky.

By the time the sky lightened to the softer gray of dawn, we reached the tree line. Fawke called another couple of hours sleep. "Another few hours of walking will take us to the original Rebel City. If it's clear, we'll make that our base camp while we find the source of our water."

We dropped backs, ate some dehydrated food, and slept. A lot of times, our missions seemed like a never-ending circle of repetition. Only the location was different.

Blackbirds cawed from the trees, disturbed by our presence. Until the army arrived in such large numbers, the Malignants had fled to the mountain in search of fresh food where deer and rabbits had been in abundance. As I drifted off to sleep, I wondered whether any of the animals were left. I'd kill for fresh venison.

I woke groggily to the tap of Fawke's foot against mine. I opened my eyes. He put a finger to his lips. I glanced at the group still in slumber. Nodding, I got to my feet and grabbed my sword, prepared to follow where he led.

He led me down a game trail. Voices drifted on the morning breeze. Fawke put two fingers to his eyes, then pointed at a gap between two branches of a low hanging tree.

Eyes wide, I peered where he pointed. Three soldiers sat around a fire, a deer roasting on a spit. No wonder I'd dreamed of venison. The aroma made my mouth water.

"Scouts?" I mouthed.

He shrugged, then jerked his head toward them.

I grinned. We were going to take their feast away from them. We hunkered down until they fell asleep. If our group woke, they'd wait for us.

Watching every placement of our feet, Fawke and I entered the clearing. I kept my sword ready as Fawke cut the venison loose. Fawke slung the carcass across his shoulders, I grabbed two rifles lying nearby, a box of ammo, and we slipped out like the wisps of smoke from their fire.

"Where have you…ah." Ezra grinned. "Scavenging."

"Found some soldiers who thought they were alone." Fawke dropped the deer on the ground. "Let's butcher this and get going. They'll come looking for it."

We'd could take the soldiers in hand-to-hand combat, but if they had more guns, they'd pick us off from the shadows. Between Fawke and Ezra, they had the meat in sections and stored in packs. We headed further up the mountain toward the location of Rebel City.

Excitement leaped in my chest at sight of the familiar path. My heart dropped as we entered what had once been a thriving mountain community. Only charred ground showed where wooden buildings had once stood. Even the barbaric fighting ring Jenkins had used to decide who would stay and who would die had been destroyed.

No smoke rose from the ashes. The army had been here a while back. While Jenkins had led his group down the mountain to us, I'd hoped this place would've been spared the wrath of Soriah. We had no safe base camp here.

Fawke led us into the trees away from the devastation. A bit further up, he took us behind thick brush and into a cave. "Found this a long time ago," he said. "We should be safe here. The foliage will disguise any signs of a fire. We'll hunt for the river tomorrow."

He moved to my side and drew me into a hug. "I'm sorry about the city. I know how much it meant to you."

"It was a semblance of a normal life." I rested my forehead on his chest.

"We'll have that one day. I promise."

I sighed and stepped back as Win handed me some venison. My stomach rumbled. We'd be well fed and rested for tomorrow when we searched for the river.

The atmosphere was almost celebratory as we ate better than we had in a long time. Maybe since I'd left Soriah as a Stalker.

"I can smoke this meat," Win said. "To preserve it. That way we can save the other rations."

"That's a good idea," I said, settling against the wall of the cave.

Already a fire warmed the stone walls and seeped into my bones. My eyelids grew heavy as I listened to the conversation around me.

Gage spoke mostly of the man she'd met, saying he might be the one. Ezra said he was too old to settle down, which caused protests from the others.

I smiled and kept eating, my gaze settling on Fawke. We enjoyed time together, our tender moments, yet he still held back from a full commitment out of fear. He didn't want my heart to break if something happened to him. It was far too late.

He smiled back, his eyes softening as his gaze dropped to my lips. I licked away the taste of venison. His brows rose as his smile widened. "Flirt," he mouthed.

"This part of the hunt I like," Jerome said, sitting next to me. "The camaraderie. I kind of like the fighting even, but those things will always scare me."

"You've seen them kill close up. Stay scared. It'll keep you alert. Get some rest. Tomorrow is another long day."

Jenkins had given us an idea of where the river might start, might wasn't completely certain since he'd had no reason to go looking for it. He'd been content with where it bubbled out of the ground near his city and provided his people with water.

We needed to do more. Block that site and protect where it originated. Without water, we'd be forced from the compound and die at the feet of Soriah's soldiers.

I stretched out, using my pack as a pillow and stared at a myriad of roots overhead that had squeezed through cracks in the rocks. I turned my head, noticing animal bones and the remnants of Malignant nests. I sniffed, their rotting odor gone from this place.

At least they hadn't cleared the mountain of animals. The soldiers had managed to break down a deer.

My eyes drifted closed, only to pop open as a twig snapped past the foliage covering our entrance. Men's voices drifted through the cave opening.

12

My fingers wrapped around my sword. My gaze locked on the entrance.

Fawke got slowly to his feet and plastered his back to the wall, his weapon held high. His gaze flicked toward me, then back.

"Well, it didn't just get up and walk away," a man outside said.

"But, we haven't seen any sign of a human in weeks. Not since we got to this mountain, anyway. They're all gone, I tell you. Since we burned that town, they have nothing to come back to."

"Then why are we here?"

"Wasting our time. I bet another animal took the deer."

"And our guns? You're an idiot."

The crunching of dried leaves signaled their passing. I released the breath I'd been holding and relaxed my shoulders. After a few minutes of silence outside, I willed myself back to sleep.

This time the rustling of my comrades preparing to set out woke me. "Why'd you let me sleep so long?" I sat up and stretched.

"You obviously needed the rest." Fawke smiled and held out a hand to help me to my feet.

"Did you get any sleep?"

"A little."

Which meant he'd gotten just enough. I didn't know how he could do what he did on so little sleep. I accepted a strip of dried meat from Win, then shouldered my pack.

Fawke studied the area outside the cave before calling the rest of us to follow. Single file, Ezra bringing up the rear, we stepped onto a well-worn trail and headed to where Jenkins thought the river flowed from the ground.

The path steepened the further we went. The air grew crisper. Black birds protested our presence from the tree branches. Once upon a time, when the sky was blue, this would have been a beautiful place. Even in the gray light, I preferred it to the city below.

A light drizzle fell from the clouds above. I couldn't help but wonder where the animals hid during the rain. The deer. The birds which were now silent. Or did their feathers and hide protect them? My mind continued to wander until Fawke stopped.

The sound of water was like music to my ears. I grinned and stepped to his side. "Can you see where it's coming from?"

"Not yet." He turned left, through the bushes and toward a large boulder jutting from the ground.

I followed. Tears sprang to my eyes at the sight of water rushing between a crevice.

Fawke dropped his pack and climbed to the top. "It's here!"

I scrambled up behind him. The water came from under another boulder and into a crevice that took it under yet another large rock. "This won't be hard to protect at all."

His eyes sparkled behind his mask. "We need to mask the sound. Won't be too hard to do with sand. Smaller rocks piled on top will hide the flow from eyes. Have them hand up rocks while I dig up sand. If we can get the rush off water sounding more like a trickle, it should be safe."

Two hours later, we had the water sounding more like a whisper. Relief that we'd found and secured our water source made my legs weak and sat on the very rock the water poured under. Fresh meat once the chickens and rabbits multiplied and our water. Our number of fighters grew one or two at a time. We had weapons and medicine. Winter rains would allow us easier access to the army camp.

Although I couldn't see Soriah, I glanced in the direction the white city stood. By springtime, we might be ready to bring the war to them.

Movement caught my attention. I narrowed my eyes, making out the forms of the soldiers whose meal we'd taken. They milled around in a clearing, clearly looking for something or someone. "Get down." I pulled at Fawke.

The rest of our group hunkered behind bushes.

I couldn't hear what the soldiers said, but it was clear they were in disagreement. Arms waved, voices rose. One whirled and marched away. The lone soldier traveled the trail we'd taken.

Casting a quick glance at Fawke, I scooted from my hiding place and joined the others. We waited, the rain stopping. The drips from tree branches sounded loud as they hit the ground.

The soldier grumbled as he climbed, talking about orders from the commander, as he stashed a radio under his poncho.

Fawke leaped from the rock, his sword inches from the man's chest. "Mind telling me what those orders are?"

The man stumbled back, falling on his rear. A whoosh of air left him. His eyes widened as the rest of us moved into his sight. "Who are you?"

"I think you know. Answer my question." Fawke touched the tip of his sword to the man's poncho.

"He's calling us down from the mountain."

"Why?"

"Our job was to see whether anymore rebels were here and to destroy the city."

"Got your answer, didn't you? Hand over the radio."

He fumbled under his poncho, emerging with the handheld radio. "Are you going to kill me?"

"Not unless I see you again." Fawke tossed the radio to me. "Tell your commander whatever you want. We won't be here by the time he sends more men. Now, go."

The man scrambled back like a crab until getting to his feet and racing down the mountain.

"Why'd you let him go?" Dante frowned.

"No sense killing him when he doesn't pose a threat."

"He'll tell the commander we're here."

Fawke shrugged. "We could be anybody up here. There's no way for them to know for sure our identity. There'll be enough killing in our future."

The radio in my hand crackled. A man's forceful voice demanded the soldiers respond. When they didn't, he cursed and hung up. The commander?

"Ready to go home?"

I thought for a minute. Win had dried out most of the deer meat after cutting it into thin strips. We had food for a few days. Could refill our drinking containers here, adding the purification tablets. "How close do you think we can get to Soriah without detection? I'd like to try and find the secret exit people are escaping from."

His eyes widened. "That's quite a trek. Dangerous, too. Are you sure?"

"If people can get out, we can get in."

"You ready to start the war?"

"No, but this would be important. What if the tunnels actually lead to the white city? If someone discovers it, they'll come for us. That's not a risk I want to take." If such a door existed, we'd have to block it off.

"That's a lot of ifs, Crynn."

"I read something in the journals that concerns me. What if the bombs seventy-five years ago weren't dropped by Soriah? What if they didn't create the Malignants, but a virus released did?"

"Who else could have?"

"Eb's father. Despite what he wrote, he couldn't have known a head of time to gather a group of people and hide in the compound. Not unless he planned the whole thing."

"Then why not take out the white city?"

"I still have a lot of reading to do, but I know the

answers are in those journals. Maybe whatever he did couldn't penetrate the dome over Soriah." I crossed my arms. Yes, it was a long shot, but one that needed taking.

"I agree with Crynn," Ezra said. "With it being the rainy season, this is the safest time for us to do this."

"Fine. We shouldn't be standing in the open. That soldier might bring the other two. Fill your water." Fawke climbed back up the rock so we could hand him our containers.

He'd come around to my way of thinking once he mulled it over. I'd spent many sleepless nights thinking the writing of Eb's father left some unanswered questions. With a couple hundred soldiers gone, space inside the white city had grown. Perhaps the reconstruction of the buildings were to house them where they were needed. It all started to make sense to me.

By the time Fawke returned to us and handed us back our containers, the creases had disappeared from his forehead. "You're right. You're the one reading the journals. I leave the next step up to you."

"Is it starting to make sense to you?"

He nodded. "Yes. Something had always seemed off to me ever since Eb told us about his father. That compound took a long time to turn into what he wanted. He had to know it was there, maybe visited that park once as a child."

"Then let's go." I bowed and waved my arm, eliciting a smile from him.

Fawke led us off the trail, through the ashes of Rebel City, and back to the waving grasses of the meadow. Soriah rose above the landscape like a beacon. Another day's hike and we'd be within range of having Lars be our eyes.

We camped in the field, miserable and cold. The radio in my pack crackled at regular intervals. The commander stated to someone that the soldiers must have perished. Since I'd spotted them crossing another field toward the camp, the commander would be surprised at the sight of them.

"There you are." Lars's voice came through my earpiece. "Took you long enough."

"Going to be even longer," I said, telling him of our plans. "Everything okay over there?"

"No. That new guy, Stan, got into a fight during training and killed someone. He's locked up waiting for you to pass judgment. Can you come back before heading out again?"

"We'll be there by day's end," Fawke said. "We'll replenish our supplies and get a good night's rest after we deal with Stan."

"Sounds good. Pick up the pace folks." We'd never had a murder before, but all punishments were the same if someone was a harm to the community. He'd be taken into the city and left to fend for himself. Most likely to perish at the hands of Malignants.

By the time we arrived, my shoulders sagged with exhaustion from our fast pace through the city. We'd skirted soldiers and small groups of Malignants since the rain had stopped. Albeit temporarily from the sight of heavy clouds overhead. Stan wouldn't last long.

Inside, I marched to the cell without dropping off

my weapons. "Wake up."

Stan sat up on the hard cot. "It was an accident."

"No, it wasn't." Samson stood from a chair in the corner. "I saw the whole thing. This rat lost a training battle. When his opponent turned, he rammed his sword through his back."

From the bruises Stan sported on his face, Samson had given him a beating. One eye swelled shut. Dried blood crusted on his lips.

I dug in my pack and pulled out a strip of dried venison. "Your last meal. In one hour, you leave."

"I'm taking my wife with me."

"No. Why would you want to subject her to a short life?" I arched a brow. "You'll be dead by morning."

He paled. "You can't mean it."

"I assure you that I do." I left and went in search of Fawke. I found him in the control room.

He turned. "We have a bigger problem. Take a look."

I stared at the monitor. Five jeeps and at least fifty soldiers marched in our direction. They'd soon be on top of us. It looked as if they were scouring every inch of the city for us. "Are we hidden well enough?"

"I sure hope so. Looks like you'll have to wait to hand out Stan's punishment. He'd run right to them."

I watched as the jeeps rumbled overhead, the sound more frightening than the bombs. The screech of what remained of the Ferris Wheel as it was slid off us sent a shudder through me. "They're going to expose the door."

"No," Lars said. "It's worse than that. The

movement blocked the door. Our only way in and out now is the large one we drove the jeeps through. That attracts attention if anyone is close."

Fawke frowned. "Looks like our search of the tunnels for an exit just took priority. We'll never move that ride from inside."

"Keep a guard on Stan at all times," I said. "The last thing we need is a murderer running loose among us."

The radio at my belt crackled. "This is Commander Sole. I demand to speak to the person in charge."

13

My gaze snapped from the radio to Fawke. "If I answer, Soriah will know I'm still alive. Right now, they only suspect."

"Call Jenkins. Let him pretend to be the leader. Let Sharon stew on that for a while."

I grinned. Jenkins and Sharon had been childhood friends before the split. Very young, but if he remembered her, she'd remember him. I nodded.

A few minutes later, Jenkins rushed into the room. After a quick explanation of what we wanted, he took the radio. "This is Jenkins."

"Jenkins who?" The commander's voice sounded more like a bark than an order. A bit on the shrill side.

"Just Jenkins. What do you want?"

"Your complete surrender."

"Won't happen. Try again."

"He's as bad ass as you," Fawke whispered, his lips tickling the hair at the nape of my neck.

I choked back a laugh.

"We're scouring the city, block by block, shoving all the debris to one end of the city. You'll have nowhere to hide. If we find you, we are ordered to shoot on sight."

"Like the soldiers did on the mountain?"

The commander cursed. "They weren't expecting to see you up there."

"Life is full of surprises. Clear the city. Saves us the job. Have fun with the monsters. Over and out."

"Don't hang up. I'm not finished."

Jenkins exhaled heavily. "What?"

"The president's aide wants to speak with you. Answer the call next time." He hung up.

"Uh, that's a turn I didn't expect," Jenkins said. "Maybe Sharon won't remember me."

"Whatever she says, you don't know where I am." I sat in a chair to the side, away from sight of the monitors.

The commander didn't waste any time contacting Sharon. The monitor flickered to life, illuminating the wall it faced. Jenkins reached over and turned it around. "I'm Jenkins, the leader here."

I cringed, knowing he'd put a target on his back at my request. To my defense, Soriah not knowing whether I was alive or dead could work to our advantage. We needed whatever upper hand we could get.

"Ah, the son of a traitor," Sharon said. "Why am I not surprised? Where is Crynn Dayholt."

"Who?" Jenkins frowned. The man could act, I'd give him that.

"Don't play coy with me. You look old."

"I could spend hours tracing the wrinkles on your face." He smirked.

"I recognize that room. I've spoken with Miss

Dayholt there. Where is she?"

"No idea. She went out a while back and never returned. I'm in charge in now."

"Her group?"

"Gone with her."

I wished I could see Sharon's face, read her expression as she processed the news.

"What is the army building?"

"Housing. We have no room for them here, and they are needed there. Where's the old man? The son of the man who built that place?"

"Dead. His heart gave out." Jenkins crossed his arms. "You've been having your share of deserters lately. Things must be bad in Soriah."

"The president has everything under control."

Jenkins laughed. "Yeah, it looks that way."

Things were quiet for a while, then Sharon spoke again. "We will find you. That place looks too large to hide for long. The army will clear the city and your location exposed."

"Then we'll fight. Are we done?"

"You're as stubborn as Miss Dayholt."

"I'll take that as a compliment." He reached over to turn off the radio, his hand pausing as she spoke again.

"You did not make the choice to leave. Your father did. We will accept you back and assign you a prominent role in the rebuilding of our great city."

"I'll take my chances here."

"Then we will repay you with the same destruction the old man's father tried on us." She clicked off.

I sent a startled glance around the room. "I was

right. Eb's father bombed this place. He created the Malignants. Not Soriah."

"Why?" Jenkins whipped to face me.

"I hope the journals will tell me. My gut tells me he wanted to rule, but didn't expect the dome over the white city to hold." I pushed to my feet. "Fawke, we hit the tunnels in an hour." I'd bet my sword Eb's father had tried digging his way to Soriah. How far had he gotten?

He gave a slow nod, clearly not liking the way I'd given the order. I mumbled a quick apology and raced to my room.

Once there, I flopped open the top journal and started skimming the pages for any clue as to what had prompted Eb's father to such a diabolical act. An act that had killed or mutated everyone living in this burned-out city. Hundreds of thousands of people. I was glad Eb hadn't lived to discover this. He'd thought his father had done a good thing.

My finger froze over a sentence half-way through the book. Eb's grandmother, too poor to receive medical treatment, had died. Blaming Soriah for their greed, Eb's grandfather had taken a group of people out. It hadn't been Eb's father after all. Now, the timeline made sense as to the falling of the bombs.

"What is it?" Fawke stood in the doorway.

"Eb's grandfather did this." I shook my head. "I can hardly comprehend the pain that would cause someone to cause such destruction."

"A broken heart makes people do a lot of things they wouldn't otherwise do."

I rested my head in my hands. "I don't ever want to grow that cold hearted."

"You won't." He stepped behind me and massaged my shoulders. "Every death pains you too much. Even the ones we cast out."

True. The decisions I made were for the better of those who lived in the compound. "What about Stan? We can't release him with the army so close. Not since we'd have to use the larger door."

"He can stay where he is for now." Fawke pulled me to my feet. "Come on. Let's get Jerome and hit the tunnels. We'll take supplies so we can stay out there as long as it takes. We'll mark our way and make a map for future use."

Since he rarely spoke so much at once, I appreciated his attempt to distract me from the turmoil in my heart. "I'm ready." I slapped the journal closed, hating the words it contained now, but knowing I'd have to read every page.

Jerome was ecstatic to be included and beamed when Fawke handed him a piece of chalk, assigning him the task of marking our way. "I'll make sure we don't go in circles." He tucked the chalk into a tiny pocket of his backpack. "And, I know, follow all orders."

"Good boy." Fawke rubbed the boy's head.

Dante met us in the supply room. "You sure you don't want more with you? No telling what you'll get into out there."

"I'm sure." I hefted my backpack to a more comfortable position. "Tell Jenkins not to answer Sharon's or the commander's call. Leave them guessing. Keep a guard on Stan. We've got our earpieces. Lars can let us know if we're needed back here."

He closed the door behind us, pitching us into an inky darkness. Seconds later, three headlamps illuminated the space in front of us.

The sound of hammering reached us before we arrived at the room where the Malignants had been. Several men had already erected walls to create more rooms. They glanced up as we passed, waved, and returned to their work.

An optimistic plan, building into the tunnels, but I really did believe we'd outgrow the compound before the final battle with Soriah. "We need someone working on restoring the electrical panel in that other room."

"That's next," Fawke said. "We'll let the workers know if we find other rooms big enough to provide housing. We also need to put lights in the tunnels before people move in. There's a lot of work to do before we can think about moving people."

Like finding out whether there actually was a way for the army to get in. Our people would be at their mercy. We had time.

We camped at the end of the day in a dead-end tunnel. Overhead, the rumble of jeeps and marching of feet dropped dirt on our heads.

"These tunnels go for miles." I stretched my legs in front of me. "Which confirms the fact Eb's grandfather wanted another way into Soriah."

"Finding the tunnel that leads that way, goes the furthest, will be tricky." Fawke lay against his pack. "I've lost all sense of direction. We could be headed toward the army camp for all I know."

"At least we can follow the marks back," Jerome said. "If we get lost. This walking and walking is boring."

I laughed. "What we're doing is important. Go to sleep." I clicked off my lamp.

"What have you done?"

I woke to a light shining in my face and an irate Herb glaring down at me. "What do you mean?"

"The commotion overhead." He leaned on his cane.

"The jeeps are clearing the city in an effort to find us. Turn off the light, please." I clicked on my lamp, putting a restraining hand on Fawke who had reached for his sword. "Your place must not be far from here if you came alone." I grinned.

His eyes widened. "Leave us alone."

"We aren't here to bother you."

"Then why are you here?"

"To find an exit to the white city."

"Isn't one. We've looked." His gaze flicked to Jerome. "Can I have the boy? We need new blood in our group."

"No." I got to my feet. "Find your own new blood." Crazy old man.

"We don't go out."

I shrugged and shouldered my pack. "We'd best be moving on. Thanks for the visit."

"You're an impertinent girl. That's why we don't want you."

"Thanks for the compliment, but I'm happy where I am." I brushed past him, a shudder ripping through me at the thought of being nothing more than a breeder.

"Be careful. There are monsters further on."

Yet, he ventured out by himself. If what he said

was true, the Malignants were getting in somehow. The tunnels were perfect for hibernation, especially with the army clearing everything out above us. The monsters had nowhere else to go. I suddenly wished we'd brought fighters with us.

An hour's walk brought us to a door. Sword in one hand, I turned the knob. The door opened onto a room of people sitting or lying on blankets. A few children drew in the dirt with sticks. While large, the place could barely hold the number of people inside. Another door stood closed on the opposite wall. Their garden and livestock?

Sonny glared. "You have no business here."

"This is where you live?" The original group's shelter before finding Rebel City had been better than this.

"This is home."

Not much of one. I stared at a very pregnant woman. The conditions were not sanitary enough to give birth. No wonder this group didn't prosper.

Herb entered behind us. "So, you found us." He let Sonny help him to a thin blanket on the ground. "What now?"

What I wanted to do was offer them room with us. The narrow-eyed glare of Herb stopped me. They might not have weapons, but this group was not to be trusted. "We leave. Good luck on birthing your baby." I backed from the room, Fawke and Jerome following me.

"That's no life," Fawke said.

"I agree, but it's one they've made and seem to prefer." I marched away from that place, amazed they'd survived as long as they had. If I could find a way to free the children from that life, I would. With us, they'd have room to play, an education, not a life of doing more than trying to increase their numbers in a space that wouldn't expand.

We rounded a corner to the sight of three Malignants, a large female and two juveniles, slipping through an open doorway.

14

I gripped my sword ready to do battle if they noticed us. "Do we follow?"

Fawke rolled his head on his shoulders. "We've taken care of three before, but…" he glanced at Jerome.

"Hey, I can fight." Jerome frowned. "You said I was good."

"Shh." My palms started to sweat. My stomach roiled. Something didn't feel right.

How could Herb wander the tunnels without fear of attack? The Malignants had entered the room ahead of her without shrieking, without glancing around, as if they had no worries.

Someone screamed, spurring us into action.

I pulled my handgun and, armed with two weapons, darted into the room.

A man lay on the dirt floor, his belly ripped open by the two juveniles feasting on him. The stench of rot stung my nostrils. The adult Malignant screeched and faced us.

I raised my gun hand and fired, dropping the

adult. The sound echoed in the room, making my ears ring. Fawke and Jerome rushed forward and disposed of the juveniles. In the distance rose the screeching of a larger number of Malignants.

"Too many for us to take on," Fawke said. "We need to find a place to hide."

"I can't tell where they are." I peered out the door, looking in each direction.

Fawke joined me and closed his eyes. "We turn right."

"How do you know?"

"Because I hear the sound of many feet coming from our left." He sprinted out, Jerome on his heels while I followed.

The hair on the back of my neck rose. I expected an attack at any moment. When we came to a T-junction, Fawke turned left. No doors greeted us on either side of the long tunnel.

"I forgot to mark our path," Jerome whispered.

"I'll remember the way." Fawke shoved the boy against the wall. "Keep your back against the dirt. If they come, we'll face them head on."

My mouth dried like the dirt at our feet. If they came, we were goners.

Shrieks rose from the direction we'd come. Screams followed.

I cast wide eyes in Fawke's direction. "Herb's group."

"We can't help them."

"They'd left that man as food for the Malignants." Bile rose in my throat. "That's why they could travel these tunnels without harm. We broke whatever truce they had with the monsters."

"Unknowingly, it appears that way." His hard gaze stayed trained on the entrance to the tunnel we hid in. "Shh."

What had happened to hibernation? The large room we'd cleared had clearly been used to sleep away the winter months. Something had changed the Malignants' behavior. The only thing I could think of was the army's arrival. They'd stirred them up and sent them underground. Soon, they'd discover where we lived and going into the tunnels in search of an exit would become too dangerous.

The attack on Herb's group was my fault. I'd shot my handgun, thus alerting the monsters. My eyes stung from tears I refused to shed. Multiple deaths lay on my shoulders. I couldn't allow myself to cry cleansing tears.

The cold of the wall at my back seeped into my skin, into my heart. Those children. The pregnant woman. I sagged.

Fawke reached out and steadied me, turning me to face him. "Stop it."

"My fault."

"No, it's theirs for forming some sort of relationship with a Malignant. We had no way of knowing. We tried to save a man we didn't know was past saving. Couldn't you smell the stink of an infection? He was dying anyway."

"That's how Herb got rid of his sick and dead."

He nodded. "Stupid way of doing things. Get your head straight, Crynn. I can't have you falling apart."

"Uh, guys." Jerome tapped Fawke's shoulder. "Do you hear that?"

Snuffles and the scraping of claws drifted toward us.

"Lights off." Fawke plastered his back against the wall and clicked off his light.

Jerome and I did the same, plunging us into darkness. Sweat poured down my back and off my brow. They'd smell us.

I gripped Fawke's hand. If I died, there was no better place than by his side.

The gentle pressure he gave back calmed me. I took a deep breath and willed my eyes to adjust to the darkness. If we perished, how long would it be before the rest of our people realized we weren't coming back. Days? A week? Maybe longer. No one knew how long it would take to search the tunnels.

I wanted electrical returned to the tunnels. Lights installed. Cameras at every junction. Unfortunately, we didn't have enough cameras, nor could I send workmen to their death installing lights. My mind whirled with all the devices that could save our life if we only had the time.

Multiple shapes moved past the mouth of our tunnel. One stopped, lifted its head and sniffed. I held my breath, praying the odor of so many Malignants in one space would mask our scent.

I tightened my hold on Fawke. My palms sweaty. I tried swallowing past the rock in my throat.

Jerome's breathing came in gasps as he tried squeezing behind Fawke. The boy's terror throbbed through me. I straightened, pulling my hand from Fawke's and taking his.

The group of Malignants moved on. My legs threatened to give out. I willed my breathing to return to normal.

After several minutes, Fawke moved to the entrance. He glanced around and waved us forward, clicking on his lamp before turning back the way we'd come.

Jerome and I did the same. Some of the tension left me as the light illuminated the darkness.

When we reached Herb's room, I wanted to ask Jerome to stay outside so he wouldn't have to see the carnage. Safety demanded he stay close.

There wasn't much left. Blood splatter covered the walls and puddled on the floor.

"Where are the children?" Not a single sign of a child. I eyed the closed door opposite us.

"Stand back." Fawke yanked open the door and jumped back.

The children, the pregnant woman, and Herb stared back at us.

"Come on out." Fawke stepped aside. "They're gone."

I knew he meant both the men and the monsters. "The woman and children will come with us."

"What about me?" Herb paled.

"We don't want your kind." Our search of the tunnels had come to an end, at least temporarily. "You're poison ideas are not allowed in our compound."

A soft cry escaped the woman at the sight of the slaughtered men. She clutched her stomach and moaned.

Oh, no. Not here. Not in the presence of so much death. "We have to get her somewhere safer, Fawke. No child should be born in…this."

Features grave, he nodded. "I don't think we'll reach Kira in time."

"Can you deliver a baby?"

"Never have. You?"

"I've seen it done, but never participated." Things had gone from bad to worse in my opinion. Birthing women made noise. A lot of noise.

"Take me with you." Herb clutched my vest. "I can deliver the baby. I know where the exit is."

I shoved him away. "We can't trust you. How could you leave that man to die like that? How do we know you won't try the same with us? You're an old, evil man who is of no use to us."

"Except for delivering the baby." Fawke, ever the voice of reason, turned to the woman. "Is he telling the truth?"

"He's delivered all the babies you see standing in front of you."

"Why are you the only woman?" And where was Sonny? Did Herb have no emotion concerning the fact his grandson no longer lived?

"I sent them in search of another place to live." Herb hitched his chin. "I saved their lives. My grandson, two men, and the rest of the women are…somewhere."

"Most likely dead, you fool." I glanced in the room where they'd been hiding. "Gather whatever you can carry. Food mostly, seeds, water. We leave in ten minutes." The old man would be locked up with Stan as soon as we returned. "Even the children can carry a pack." I moved to keep guard at the doorway while Fawke supervised the others.

Our chances of returning home had been

drastically reduced. The woman's breathing came hard and fast. I turned as her water broke. The baby would be born among death after all. "Move her into the other room."

Herb ushered the women and children back into their storage room. He gently helped her lie down. "Bite on this." He handed her a worn piece of leather. "You must not scream."

I closed the door, grateful it would muffle some of the noise, and glanced around for clean rags and a way to heat water. I found rags not exactly clean and only cold water. The baby would have a chilly start to his or her life.

"I can't watch this." Fawke turned away.

"You've never witnessed a birth? Not even an animal?"

"No." He shuddered. "Right now, I'd rather be anywhere but here. Even out there with the Malignants. At least then I'd know what to do."

Despite the severity of our situation, I couldn't stop from smiling. "Big, brave, Fawke, brought to his knees by the birth of a baby."

"It isn't funny." His lips twitched.

"I'll assist Herb. You stay over there with Jerome. He looks a bit traumatized."

"I am not." Jerome crossed his arms. "This doesn't scare me near as much as seeing that large group did. A baby isn't going to try and eat me."

"At least turn around and give this poor woman some privacy."

Herb had shoved her dress to her waist. "Deep breaths, Camille. This isn't your first time. Your new baby will come quickly."

Although I disliked the man, he did seem to know what he was doing and didn't require help from me. I sat against the wall and worked on formulating a plan on getting us out of there alive.

While Herb delivered a baby, the children harvested vegetables, shoving them into sacks they could sling over their shoulders. The quiet way they worked had me wondering whether they'd ever had the opportunity to run and play, to laugh with each other. The oldest, a girl who looked to be about twelve, whispered instructions to the others. When they'd finished, cages of rabbits and chickens piled against the wall, they sat in a semi-circle around me.

I bit my lip and returned their stares. After a while, I squirmed under their scrutiny. "What?"

"We've never seen a woman like you before," the oldest girl whispered.

Could she speak above a whisper? "You'll be seeing a lot of new things."

"Like what?" A young boy leaned forward, also speaking in a whisper. "I want to fight like him." He pointed at Jerome.

"How old are you?"

He shrugged. "We don't do that here."

He looked about ten to me, but could be older considering he'd been down here his whole life with no chance of proper growth and stimulation. "What are your names?"

"We don't have names. Herb calls us boy or girl."

"That won't do at all. I'm Crynn, and that is Fawke and Jerome. The woman having a baby has a name."

"There are too many to bother with names," Herb

said. "Ah. A baby boy." He held the newborn high for everyone to see.

"I want to name him Freedom," Camille said. "We're no longer bound by your rule. You sent my Sonny out there to die." She sat up and snatched the baby from Herb's hands. Now, they can send you away."

Herb scowled. "Not if they want to know where the exit to this place is."

Fawke stood over the old man. "I'll kill you if I find out you're lying to us. If you know of the exit, why live the way you do?"

"There's nothing but death above ground."

"You've brought the same down here by offering your sick and dying to those things. If we're discovered on our way back, I'll cut you and leave you the same way you did that man. I will not risk my people for you." Fawke took a deep breath through his nose. "Everyone carries a pack and a crate, except for Camille. Her job is keeping her baby quiet. Any noise could get us killed."

15

We made too much noise. The shifting of packs and animal crates, the shuffling of feet, the whimpers from the baby. Camille nursed the poor thing every time it made a sound, but I wasn't sure it was enough.

My heart beat in my throat so hard I thought the sound could be added to the noise around us. I glanced over my shoulder wanting to tell them to run, to breathe quieter, anything.

The solemn expression on Fawke's face did nothing to dispel my unease, nor did his constant checking behind us.

I glared at Herb. The old man flinched. He'd put us in this precarious position. Us and the children. I could care less about his wrinkled hide.

It took two days to reach the room where our men worked. I almost cried tears of relief to see them unharmed. Noticing weapons close at hand, I relaxed more. We were almost home.

I admired the noncomplaining of the children and Camille. They showed a strength I wouldn't have believed if I hadn't seen it with my own eyes, walked two days by their side.

The door to the compound swung open at our approach. Ezra's eyes widened. "You are full of surprises, Crynn."

"Malignants killed most of their group. Have Kira check out the children and the woman. Get them cleaned up, fed, and housed. Put the old man in the cell with Stan. Send guards to watch over the workmen."

"About Stan…"

I narrowed my eyes. "What happened?"

"He escaped. Conked Dante over the head pretty good." He held up a hand to stop my questions. "He's alright. Kira has him in the infirmary recovering from a concussion."

"Where is Stan now?"

"Incinerator." He shrugged and bolted the door. "Jenkins thought it best we dispose of him. This place doesn't need a volatile man."

"The army?"

"Moved on."

"Let's take these people to the infirmary," Fawke said. "We can catch up later. Can you take care of the old man, Ezra?"

"Yep." He gave Herb a shove. "No idea what you did, man, but if Crynn wants you locked up, it must be bad."

The shrieking of Malignants came from the other side of the door. My blood chilled. Those things had followed our trail. I tossed a glance at Fawke.

"Two minutes. Ezra, hurry." Fawke raced away. Seconds later, his voice came over the intercom.

"Every available fighter to the armory now."

I turned to Jerome, taking note of the exhaustion on his face. "I need you to take these people to the infirmary. It's important that you take charge of them." I put my hand on his shoulder, knowing he'd rather fight. "The little ones look up to you. Give them names, show them around. Will you?"

"Yes." He squared his shoulders and led them away.

Despite my own weariness, I raced to the armory where twenty had gathered, including Dante and Kira. "No, Dante. You've been injured."

"I'm good." He set his jaw and shot Kira a look.

"He's capable of fighting." She hooked a gun belt on her hip. "Rory is looking after the woman and the children. What's important now is our men out there."

"The Malignants are between them and us."

"Uh, Crynn." Lars spoke over the intercom. "Those monsters are scratching at the door. Literally."

"How many?"

"About fifteen."

"Get everyone who won't be fighting into the training room and lock the doors."

His warning rang out a second later. The pounding of feet showed that our people hadn't hesitated to follow his instructions.

"We congregate in the supply room." Fawke stood in front of us. "The door will be bolted behind us. We'll meet the Malignants head on. Not one of them can get by us. Not a single one. Since there are too many of us to fight effectively in that room, I want ten of you to join the people in the training room. They will need protection."

Eight men and two women left the armory, weapons in hand. The rest of us sprinted for the supply room.

Nails on steel sent shivers through me. The slamming of the door behind us chilled my blood. Instead of forming our normal fighting circle, we stood in a straight line a few feet apart.

A man I didn't know unbolted the door.

It crashed open, pinning him behind it.

Battle cries joined the shrieking of the beasts as we held our ground. They charged, fangs bared.

One of our newer fighters shrank back, fear etched on her face.

"Do not fall," I ordered. "Fight for your family."

I jabbed, slashed, and lunged. Every thought left me as I fought on automatically, the moves as natural as breathing. My training spurred me on as one Malignant after another fell.

The frightened woman next to me stumbled backward under the onslaught of a large male Malignant. Her scream rose above the sounds of battle. I turned and buried my sword in the back of his neck, then upward into what brain the creature possessed.

Seeing the woman still lived despite the savage wound on her side, I ordered her to seek shelter behind some crates and returned to the battle. Slowly, we pushed the monsters back into the tunnel where we had more room to fight. There, we formed our fighting circle and disposed of them.

I sagged against the wall. "How many did we

lose?"

"The man behind the door and one more." Fawke leaned by my side. "We have to find out how they're getting in."

"Considering how slow Herb is, it will take days. We'll have to take a large group in case we run up against Malignants." My breathing slowly returned to normal. "But you're right. We need to keep these beasts out of the tunnels. Usually, winter kept them dormant."

"There is nothing usual since the army arrived. Not to mention Herb feeding these things. They now think the tunnels are a buffet." He pushed away from the wall. "Let's get some rest. We'll have to head out soon. Send someone to check on our workers."

As the adrenaline wore off, a heavy cloak of fatigue covered me. I shuffled to the showers, more grateful than I could express that our people were safe. At least for the time being.

I stepped under the hot spray of water and turned, letting the water flow over my head and down my back, washing away the blood and stench of the Malignants. The water swirling down the drain turned red.

For once, I didn't rush my shower, not worried about wasting water. If I could've fallen asleep there, I would have. Finally, I realized that we might not run out of water, but only a certain amount stayed heated, and others would need to wash away the filth of battle.

I turned off the faucet and donned loose-fitting clothes. My stomach ached from too long without food. Revived a bit, I headed for the dining room instead of my room.

Jerome sat with the children, smiling as I approached them. "They've never seen such things, Crynn. Can you believe it? Not even a plate. I'm going to be busy teaching them all I know."

"They are very lucky to have you." I grabbed a plate of my own and joined Dante at a table. "What happened?"

"It's embarrassing." He hung his head. "I stepped close to the cell to give Stan his meal. He grabbed my shirt and yanked me against the bars, stunning me. Then, he took the keys from my belt and beat the living crap out of me once he freed himself. Ezra found me, took me to the infirmary, then searched for Stan. He found him in the showers. All I know after that is Jenkins ordered him killed. I'm sorry."

"Accidents happen. At least he didn't kill you."

"You've had a rough few days, too, it seems."

I nodded and filled him in on Herb's group. "He doesn't seem to care whether his grandson and the others are alive or not."

"If they are, they'll come here. Do you believe the old man knows where the entrance is?"

"Let's say I'm skeptical." Doubtful to tell the truth. I think Herb stalled so we wouldn't release him alone into a world he feared.

Jenkins entered the room. Spotting me, he sat next to me. Dante excused himself and left.

"Thanks for taking care of things in my absence." I spooned some peas into my mouth.

"If you keep bringing in strays, we'll run out of food and room." He crossed his arms.

"I'm working on making sure that doesn't

happen. I'll take in anyone that seeks sanctuary here."

"I've never thought you a fool until now."

"Look. We took you in. If you don't like the way I run things, then leave."

"That would be suicide."

"Then you've decided. I'd like to eat in peace, please." I didn't have the patience to argue with a man who used to make people fight to the death in order to join him. That made him marginally better than Herb in my opinion. But, he did know how to lead and could step in when Fawke and I were away.

My hand froze halfway to my mouth. Would he try to take over on a permanent basis? I needed to find Fawke.

I rushed from the dining room and banged on his door. A groggy Fawke answered. "What's wrong?"

"I think Jenkins is going to try and out me as leader."

"Impossible. The people won't go for it."

"Those who came with him might." I closed the door behind me, averting my gaze from his shirtless torso. Well, tried to. My gaze kept drifting back.

"Am I making you uncomfortable?" He gave a crooked grin. "I can put a shirt on."

"It's your room." I swallowed hard. "What are we going to do about Jenkins?"

"I'll feel him out. Maybe it's as simple as involving him more in the decision making. Get some sleep, Crynn." He stepped in front of me, placing a tender kiss on my lips. "Go to your room before we do something we'll both regret. We have a lot of traveling to do soon, and you're so tired, you're about to fall over." He cupped my cheek. "Unless you want to stay with me?"

Temptation reared, but that was a step I shouldn't take. I already cared way too much for this man. Until the threat of Soriah was over, I couldn't make that move. "Goodnight," I whispered, leaving.

In my room, I stretched out on the bed and stared at the ceiling. Enemies surrounded me, both at home and outside. The only ones I could truly rely on were Fawke and the rest of the original group. Sometimes, I almost wished for the days back when it was just the seven of us.

16

Fawke and Jenkins waited for me at breakfast. I cast them a wary look as I picked up a bowl from the sideboard, then joined them.

"What has the two of you so serious this morning?" I sat and stared at my meal. Was that an egg? A real egg on top of the oatmeal like substance?

"Fawke told me that you think I'm trying to oust you as leader?" A pained look crossed Jenkins's face.

"It seems that way from our conversation yesterday." I really didn't want anything like an angry confrontation to spoil my enjoyment of a special treat at breakfast.

"Just because I don't always agree with what you're doing doesn't mean I want your job. I'm perfectly happy pretending for those in Soriah."

I tore my gaze away from the egg. "That's good to know. I propose a committee that meets to make major decisions. We'll start with the three of us." I couldn't wait any longer. I cut into the egg and popped half into my mouth, closing my eyes at the taste I'd missed so much.

"I propose our core group plus Jenkins here." Fawke chuckled. "Never saw someone so happy over an egg."

"Might be the last one I get for a while. We've got to head out again. It'll be a slow trip with Herb along. Do you think he'll draw us a map?" I opened my eyes.

"Doesn't hurt to ask." Fawke got to his feet. "I'll be back."

"I'm sorry if I came across harsh." Jenkins shoved his bowl my way. "Have my egg. You're too skinny."

"I don't think an egg will fatten me up, but thanks." I ate it before he changed his mind. "We'll have the radio from the commander. There's another in the storage room. We'll be out of range to hear from Lars. Contact us on channel two if something comes up."

"How many will you be taking?"

"The original group, plus others to make a total of twenty. Keep the workmen guarded. Have them install more cameras at junctions in the tunnel and get those machines working in the second room. Keep the people training. Is the exit door still blocked?"

He nodded. "The army has been too active for us to get out the larger door. When we can, we'll have to clear the door, but keep it looking as if it's blocked, if that makes sense. We'll make it a priority once it's clear to do so." He arched a brow. "That it?"

"I think so. Use your judgment." Finished, I stood and held out my hand. "Thank you for being on my team."

Smiling, he returned the handshake. "Forgive me for calling you a fool. I know you're preparing for future refugees. You've done more since arriving here than I did building Rebel City. The wheel chose right. You're a born leader."

Pride filled me. I had taken to the role despite not wanting it. Before locating Fawke, I headed to the kitchen to see my mother.

"Leaving again?" She turned from washing dishes.

"Yes. I came to say goodbye. I don't know how long we'll be gone."

She dried her hands and wrapped me in a hug. "You'll be fine. You're stronger than I ever imagined you would be." Stepping back, she cupped my face. "Come back to me."

"I'll have my people with me. We've encountered much worse than a tunnel full of Malignants. Please have the kitchen staff supply us with enough provisions for twenty people for a week." I gave a shaky smile and stepped back. "When I return, we'll have found another way out of here." We'd use the door large enough for jeeps, but it lowered and rose so slowly, the risk of being seen outweighed the need to open it unless we had to.

Fawke met me in the hall. "The old man says he only knows the way, not how to draw a map."

I exhaled heavily. "No choice but to take him. Let's gather our twenty in the armory. The kitchen will bring us enough supplies for a week."

Jerome waited for us at the armory. He held up a hand before I could tell him he wasn't coming this time. "I know you need me, but I'm staying here. The new kids need me more than you do."

Nodding, I smiled. "Wise choice. They depend on you, and if things go bad here, this place needs a fighter like you."

"That's what I thought. Good luck." He clapped me on the shoulder, then left.

"I really like that kid," Fawke said, getting into his riot gear before shoving his rubber suit into a bag that would hang from his pack.

"You're optimistic that we'll find the exit, aren't you?"

"Best to be prepared." He gave a lopsided grin. "It is winter. If we go out, it could be raining. Plus, I really want to go up. It seems like we've been underground forever."

I agreed. The thought of traveling days through the tunnels didn't hold much appeal.

Outfitted, we stepped into the hall to allow room for the others to enter. Already packs were lined against the wall with our supplies.

"I feel so loaded down," Kira said, "that movement will be difficult." She had not only a bag with her rubber suit, the backpack of supplies, but also a bag of medical. "I've attached clips that I can press a button and the bags drop."

"Genius. We could all use those."

She handed me a box. "A step ahead of you. If we encounter a large group of Malignants, we can't afford to be weighed down."

This was why I preferred the original seven. Strong minds with each of them. They made up for areas I lacked.

I clipped the army radio to my belt. "Let's get

moving." I turned and headed to the tunnel door.

Citizens of Rebel City lined the way, clapping as we passed, and sending up prayers for our protection. While almost impossible we would all return, I knew the Supreme Being could make it happen.

Jenkins waited to open the door for us. "God speed."

Herb stood, leaning on his cane. "Just so you know, I won't hold you back. I've still got some strength in me, although I feel in my bones that I'll die out there."

"Don't cast a shadow over us." I glared.

"Hush, old man." Gage shook her head. "Crynn should have left you out there. We'd have found the tunnel exit somehow."

"Hmm." He stepped out the door.

Foreboding lowered on my shoulders like a heavy shroud. The optimism I'd felt by the support of my people slipped away.

Fawke shook his head. "Don't go there, Crynn. Keep your head in the game. This won't be an easy mission, but it isn't an impossible one."

"Stop reading my mind." I smiled. He always could bring me back into focus. I followed Herb into the tunnels, the others behind me.

Without Jerome with us, Dante took over the task of marking our way, drawing arrows showing the way back.

Halfway through the third day, we approached an open door. At least I thought it was the third day. Time was easily lost there.

"This is how the monsters get in." Herb leaned against the wall, his breath coming in gasps. "The latch is broken."

"Where does it lead?" My nose wrinkled against the odor of rot.

"Sewers."

"How far do these tunnels go?"

He grinned. "Under the entire city. I've spent my life traversing them. Never had any trouble until those things found a way in."

"Sewers," Fawke repeated. "They go everywhere. We can get close to the army, Soriah, anywhere we want."

"Once we clear them of Malignants," Ezra said.

"We have before." I remembered fighting in the dark the first week I arrived. Clearing the sewers would give us a huge advantage. "It'll be a tough and dangerous job. Herb, you head back."

"Alone?" He frowned, adding more wrinkles to his face.

"I can't spare a fighter. Be cautious and quiet. It's nothing you haven't done before."

"So, I will die out here."

"Most likely." Harsh, but true. I couldn't risk lives by moving at his slow pace through the sewers. "Thank you for being truthful about the exit."

His shoulders sagged. "I'll leave in the morning."

I located a fist-sized rock and jammed it against the base of the door to keep it closed. "We'll rest and head out in a few hours. Eat and drink, everyone. You'll need your strength."

A nudging of my foot woke me. I opened my eyes to the grave expression of Fawke.

"The old man is dead." He jerked his head to where Herb slumped against the wall. "In his sleep. I think the last three days were too hard on him."

I rubbed the back of my neck. At least I no longer had to send him to his death. I got up and stood over him. He'd kept his word after all. We owed him a debt we could never repay. "If his body is still here when we return, we'll take him back with us." Rest in peace you crotchety old man. "I wonder where Sonny is."

"We've seen no sign of them. Maybe they went up."

"Without weapons? It would be suicide."

He shrugged. "They didn't strike me as being very bright. If they did make the attempt, I doubt they made it out of the sewers. Staying removed from the world above for so long did them no favors."

"Let's get the others up." I pulled Herb's robe over his face, said a prayer, and then gathered my things. I didn't like the old man, appreciated his sacrifice, but wouldn't mourn. How many of his people had died at the hands of Malignants because of his backward ways?

Once the noise of putting our gear back on quieted, I removed the rock and swung the door open. The foul odor slapped me in the face. If not for the riot shield blocking some of it, I might have keeled over.

I stepped into inches of sludge left behind by humans long since passed. A little better than wading knee deep in the stuff. I glanced left, right, then left again. Having gotten turned around in the tunnels, I had no idea in which direction to go. Remembering Fawke saying to always go right to keep from getting lost, I turned in that direction.

"I sure hope we aren't camping down here in this stuff," a man behind me said.

Fawke assured him we'd go up to rest. "No more talking. Sound carries."

At least the sludge muffled our footsteps. I breathed through my mouth, taking shallow breaths.

We hadn't encountered anything living other than rats by the time we reached the first ladder rising to the top. Fawke took the lead, slowly raising the cover. After a few seconds, he motioned for us to start climbing.

I went up last, alert for any sign of danger. As I waited, I realized if Malignants could climb, then they could learn to open doors. Something or someone had broken the latch on the door to the tunnels. I didn't think it had been Herb or one of his people. That door allowed danger to enter their world, a world closed off to all but themselves.

Fawke knocked on the ladder, pulling me from my thoughts. I climbed to join the rest and spoke softly telling Fawke of my musings.

"They are getting smarter. There was a time no one thought they'd breed. Now look at them. Like rats."

"Where are we?" I studied a landscape different from before because of the bombings and the army clearing the debris. The only shelter was a building with no windows. Rebar rose from the structure.

"I don't know yet. When we go back down in the morning, I'll write a description of the place on the wall. If we ever have to flee into the sewers, we need to know where every manhole leads. Let's camp here and see whether we can get to a high enough point in that building to determine where the army camp is. I do know we're too close to Soriah for my comfort."

Which meant we were quite a way from the army. I turned around. The white city stood stark against a dark sky.

17

Keeping low, Fawke led us to the closest building and away from sight of Soriah. Once inside the dust-filled space, I released a sigh of relief. I didn't have to see to know that Soriah would have posts on its walls.

"What's next?" Ezra sat and stretched his legs out in front of him. "Soriah or the army camp? If we would have gone left, the sewer might have led us right inside the white city."

"This is a scouting mission only." Fawke frowned. "We aren't ready to start the war. We'll kill Malignants if we run across them, clearing the sewers, but will not engage with the army unless we have no other choice. Crynn?" He motioned to a set of winding stairs.

I nodded and followed, curious to see where we'd come up in regard to the compound. Although the top half of the building had been blown to pieces, we were able to get high enough to see a good distance.

What remained of our Ferris Wheel could barely be seen in the pile of rubble the army had pushed it into. Further away, I could barely make out the white tents of the army camp. In another direction, the mountain that held our water source rose. More mountains broke up the landscape now that more buildings had fallen.

I narrowed my eyes at the jagged…something in the distance. "Is that another city?"

Fawke held binoculars to his eyes. "I'll be damned." He handed them to me. "Now that most buildings here are down, we can see a lot farther. Yes, that's another city."

"Do you think there are people?" I raised the binoculars.

The far-off city looked as destroyed as the one where we are had been when I arrived. The army either didn't care about any survivors because they weren't causing trouble or there weren't any.

"How far do you think it is?" I handed the eyepiece back.

"At least a week's march, maybe more. There's a lot of open ground between here and there."

"We'd have to travel at night."

He cut me a glance. "You want to go there, why?"

"People. If we're here, there is a good possibility people live there, too."

"It could be a total waste of time. We need to clear the tunnels before considering such a thing."

"You're right." I couldn't help but wonder whether there was a way to communicate with possible survivors. Eb's grandfather had really wanted no one around while he tried to overpower Soriah. He'd wanted no challenges. If not survivors from his dirty bombs, the place would be crawling with Malignants.

"You need to realize we might never have an army big enough to face Soriah." Fawke's words cut straight to my heart.

I refused to lose hope. I didn't want my entire life to be one of living underground in hiding. Rather than respond, I headed back down the stairs.

In the morning, we headed back to the sewers. Fawke sent glances my way now and then, but didn't break my silence. Obstinate or not, I wanted his support, not always his voice of reason. I would free the people from the overbearing rule of President Cane. Somehow.

"What's wrong with you two?" Ezra fell into step beside me. "The air is chillier this morning."

I whispered about the other city and Fawke's reluctance to make the trip. "If we don't find a large group to join us instead of waiting for a couple at a time to trickle in, I'll die of old age before Cane is brought down."

"Both of you are right, but that will be a harrowing journey. What if the survivors, if there are any, are not friendly? Can we risk our fighters? Think on it long and hard, little girl. You know we'll follow you to the ends of the earth if you ask. Just make sure it's worth the asking."

I got it. The two men I respected the most believed it a fool's quest. "I'll let it go."

Fawke held up a closed fist in a signal for us to stop. Something clattered further in the darkness. The noise too loud to have been made by a rat.

I strained my ears to hear signs of Malignants.

They weren't usually concerned with silence when prey was around. When Fawke clicked off his light, the rest of us did the same.

Even after my eyes adjusted to the darkness, visibility was slight. A shadow passed where we stood, followed by another, then another. Not monsters, but human. They didn't seem weighed down with weapons as soldiers would be.

I ran the hilt of my sword on the wall, the scratching sound it made echoing.

"Who's there?" A startled voice came from around the bend.

"Sonny?" I widened my eyes. "Come here."

Minutes later, four shadows stood in front of us. I flicked on my light.

Sonny threw a hand in front of his eyes. "You blinded me."

"Is this all that's left of you?"

"No. We're hunting rats for food."

My gaze flickered to the iron bar in his hand. "Your people are with us now. Maybe you should join them."

"My grandfather? Camille?"

"Died in his sleep. Camille has a healthy baby boy. Where's the rest of your group?"

"My heart is sad to hear of his passing. We're in a garage aboveground. There's ten of us. We take turns coming down here."

"How have you avoided the Malignants?"

"They can't smell us over the stuff we're standing in."

He was smarter than I gave him credit for. "Lead the way."

Sonny turned and headed right and up a ladder. Up top, he sprinted across a weed-covered road and into a sagging metal building.

We barged into the sight of ragged, smelly people roasting rats on sticks over a fire. They glanced up in alarm.

"It's fine." Sonny held up his hands. "The rest of our people are in their compound. We're welcome there."

Another small group to join us. They weren't trained fighters, but they were brave, I'd give them that. They could be trained to fight.

Fawke gave them directions to the compound. "It'll take you at least two days. We'll radio ahead that you're coming."

"Would you like something to eat?" One of the women held out a roasted rat.

"No, thanks." I shuddered, not wanting to eat another one for a very long time. "Have you encountered many Malignants in the sewers?"

"Sometimes," Sonny says. "We lay low until they pass. The soldiers march by once in a while, but I think our stench keeps them away."

"No large patrols?"

He shook his head. "Just a few at a time. That's why we've camped on the edge. It's away from the camp and the rebuilding."

"Be safe. When you reach the compound," I said, "find a man named Jenkins. He'll get you cleaned up and fed properly. The next day, all of you will begin training. The fact you've survived out here without proper weapons shows you have what's needed to make a soldier. One more thing. Why did you separate from your group?"

"To find out where the sewers led."

"Let's go. We've a few hours before stopping for the night." Fawke headed back out.

We again dashed across the open lot and back into the dark. Why had Herb cared where the sewers went since he had no desire to leave his crowded two-room home? He had to have known the risk he'd put Sonny and the others in.

I must have voiced my thoughts out loud, because Fawke answered. "I think they were planning on moving out of the tunnels."

"They were safer underground."

"It had been so long since he was up here, he wanted to make sure."

Made sense, sort of. I clicked my headlamp on as Sonny's group came down the ladder and headed in the opposite direction.

We continued trudging through sludge. Knowing the foul odor provided us some protection, it didn't bother me as much, and I'd gotten used to rats a long time ago.

We climbed up and down ladders, taking note of our surroundings, before coming out into a small courtyard surrounded by brush and a sagging fence. Fawke called a halt to camp.

I dropped to the ground in a thud, shrugging out of my pack and glancing at the sky. No threat of rain, but the courtyard did offer an overhang to protect us if the weather changed.

"All this walking is overrated," a man named Tomas said. "How long are we going to do this?"

"Until we've scoured all of the tunnels." Fawke

shook his head. "Crynn, let's climb that pile of rubble and take a look. The rest of you eat and get some rest."

We climbed just high enough to be able to see over. We were closer to the army camp, but in a section of the city that didn't look familiar.

"I'm sorry." Fawke's gaze softened. "I don't want to be unsupportive."

"It's okay. I know it was a silly thought and a waste of time." I lifted the binoculars to my eyes.

Five Malignants dug through a trash heap. "The army is dumping its garbage. They're asking for the Malignants to attack."

"Keeps those things from sniffing us out."

"I'd take it further from camp, though." I handed him the binoculars. "Have we been here before?"

He laughed. "This is where you were dropped. Looks a bit different after all the bombings."

That day seemed a lifetime ago. I landed an innocent eighteen-year-old. Now, at nineteen, I felt as old as Eb some days. "The interior of the city has been decimated, but there are a lot of buildings around the perimeter to rebuild. It will take Cane's lifetime to accomplish." Talk about a waste of time.

"Not if they only do enough to house the army. My guess is they'll keep the civilians in the white city under their control."

Hmm. I rolled to my back and stared at the clouds overhead wondering whether the sky that had once been blue had been portrayed accurately in the books I'd read. Would the sun ever burn off the gray left behind by the dirty bombs? Trees and weeds grew, so at least some light got through.

None of us were dying from vitamin D deficiency. But, I sure would like to see something more than gray and black.

"What are you thinking?" Fawke continued to scan the horizon.

"About a blue sky and white clouds. Rain you could dance in. Flowers, rainbows, and bright-colored birds."

"Fantasizing."

"Yeah."

"I'm glad you still can. I've seen the stress on your face more often than not." He turned and lay next to me, taking my hand. "Let's stay here a while. It's hard to find time alone with you where we aren't solving problems or making plans.

A Malignant shrieked off in the distance. Not close enough to warrant a feeling of danger. Not while Fawke held my hand. Other than that, the night was silent. In my mind, white, fluffy clouds drifted by, playing peek a boo with the moon. I smiled remembering all the times my mother said I kept my head in the clouds and not my feet on the ground.

Keeping my feet on the ground wasn't all that pleasant. I turned my head, bringing my face inches from Fawke's. My gaze fell to his lips, then…was that a white cloud?

"Fawke, look."

He lifted the binoculars to his eyes. "That's smoke coming from that faraway city."

18

Question about other survivors answered. Unless Soriah had soldiers way over there, which I doubted. "What do we do now?"

"Keep traveling the sewers. We'll worry about that city later." Fawke lowered the binoculars. "Makes me wonder why Eb didn't say anything about all the branches forking out from our compound."

"Maybe they left Soriah on their own recently."

"True, but most have come searching for us. Why go so far away?"

I shrugged. "Maybe they left before we rebelled and don't know we exist." I couldn't help but wonder whether they had weapons. How did they survive the Malignants if they didn't? That city could hold a world of possibilities for us in means of supplies. If the army, or Soriah's scouts, hadn't ventured that far, there could be things there to benefit us.

Shaking off thoughts of taking what belonged to others, I climbed from the debris. It's quite possible those people had been living there for years. Who was I to take anything from them? All I could do was ask them to join us. If they refused, we'd walk away, praying they didn't come to take what was ours.

The next morning, we went back to the tunnels and closer to the army camp if my sense of direction was correct. Fawke climbed a ladder and opened the grate at the top. "Get back!" He scrambled down as the shriek of several Malignants reached my ears.

The beasts didn't bother climbing down, but simply leaped into the sludge. Five of them soon advanced on us as we tried to back up, hampered by twelve people crowded into a narrow sewer.

"Dante, the flame thrower," Fawke said.

"It'll alert the army. Fire is going to go up the manhole."

"Just do it. Everyone else duck."

I fell belly first into the slime as Dante rested the flame thrower on his shoulder. The first blast took out three of the Malignants and shot the manhole cover into the air. I scrambled to my feet and helped Fawke dispose of the other two.

Minutes later, shouts and pounding feet sent us racing in the opposite direction.

"There are several dead…things down there. Burned to a crisp. Gas leak maybe?" A man's voice drifted down the sewer.

"I guess it severed that one's head, too. You're an idiot. Someone is down there."

"Do we follow?"

"They have a flame thrower. We alert the commander."

Fawke pounded his fist against his thigh. "We had no other choice. We couldn't win against the

Malignants down here. We don't have the footing in this stuff they do. Head back to the next ladder. We can't be caught down here."

We raced back as quickly as we could. My feet threatened to slip several times to drop me back into the grime. Thankfully, the riot gear had kept it off my face.

At the ladder, we rushed up. Fawke searched for a place to hold up. "That building."

A small structure stood intact across a large empty space. If we hurried, we could make it before the army swarmed the place.

Weighed down by supplies and a rubber suit, I started to fall back from Fawke, Ezra, and Dante. When they slowed, I waved them on. "I'll make it." There were others not as fast under their burdens.

Fawke refused to leave me, slowing until I caught up. "I'll never leave you behind." He repeated the words once we reached the safety of the building.

"I'll never be far." My gaze locked on his until the rumble of a jeep pulled us apart.

"Further into the building," Fawke said. "Quickly and quietly."

"I thought those things couldn't smell us with sewer covering us," Moses said.

"I lifted the manhole cover in the middle of them. It came up right where the army dumped their garbage." Fawke raced down a hallway to a room at the back of the building.

A woman next to me stopped, shaking her head. "We're sitting ducks here. I can't." She whirled and darted back outside.

I raced after her.

Rapid gunfire cut her down the second she emerged from the building. Bullets ripped into her, spinning her like a dust devil until she fell. She'd given us away.

"Crynn!" Fawke ordered me back. "Back door."

I hurried back to the others. We burst out a back door toward another building. Once, we'd been able to outrun the jeeps. Not anymore. Not since they'd cleared the streets. Voices rose from a man cover as we sprinted past. The army was now below and behind us.

My blood chilled as a helicopter appeared on the horizon. "We've got to get inside."

"Working on it," Fawke said. "Here." He ducked into a building that looked as if it would collapse at any minute. Bent over, I followed him through a maze of iron and concrete. With nineteen of us, the going was tight and slow.

My breath came in gasps. I'd lived underground for months, but now I became claustrophobic with the crowding in on me. Spots darted in front of my eyes. I blinked, focusing on the sight of Fawke's strong back leading the way.

He squeezed through a narrow opening. Trying to control my breathing, I followed, finding myself in a breezeway between two buildings. Instead of entering the other building, Fawke turned, staying close to the back wall.

The area was just big enough for all of us. Other buildings rose above us.

"They can't see us from the air, and we aren't in any of the buildings. This is the safest place right now." He stared through a tangle of rebar overhead as the helicopter passed. "Get a drink and something to eat while you can. We may have to flee at any time. If we have to fight, use your firing weapons. Swords will be of no use against the army's guns."

He put a hand on my shoulder. "You okay?"

"I didn't like being in there." I took a deep breath. "Felt too much like a burial."

He flashed a grin. "We don't bury. We burn."

I rolled my eyes. "Smart aleck." I rummaged in my back for a dry bar made of rat and vegetables. Tasteless, but filling. After I ate, I washed it down with a few sips of purified water.

In the distance came the sounds of the army searching for us. The jeep tires over stone, the circling helicopter, the shouts of men. How long would they search before giving up?"

The radio on Fawke's belt crackled.

"This is your commander. Update status."

"No sign of them, sir. Maybe the woman was alone."

"One woman brought down five of those things? Are you serious?" His voice rose. "Did you find a fire launcher on her? There are more of them."

"They aren't in the sewers," another man said. "All clear here. They're up top somewhere."

"Then move up top. Search every building until they're found." An audible click signaled the commander hanging up.

"What now?" I asked. "They'll find us eventually."

"Back to the sewers. You heard the man. We aren't there." He shrugged his pack into place. "We'll find a manhole out of sight of the soldiers and enter there. Everyone stay here until I return. One person will be less noticeable. I'll be back once I know the safest place to go back in."

His gaze warmed as it landed on me. "If I'm not back in thirty minutes…"

"You will be."

He pressed his lips together and nodded.

I wanted to beg him to stay. The last time he'd left me, he'd been captured and whipped. His back would carry the scars for the rest of his life. But I realized the wisdom in his going alone and nodded.

When he'd gone, I turned to the others. "Dante, you guard our entrance with the launcher. Anything or anyone other than Fawke that we can't take down easily, you dispose of."

"It'll give away our position again."

"If they come here, they've already discovered us." I leaned against the wall, doubting anyone would come through the tight maze we had squeezed through. It never amazed me how Fawke could find such a place.

"Is this what Stalkers used to do?" A man named Grayson asked. "This isn't the life for anyone. All this running and fighting."

"Yes, this pretty much sums up what we used to do," Ezra said. "Can't say this old body misses it much."

"You thinking about hanging up your hat?" Gage asked, grinning. "Always thought you'd fight until your last breath."

"Oh, I will as long as these legs will carry me."

"You kept up with Fawke just fine. Unlike me." I returned my water bottle to my pack.

"Your legs are too short." He laughed. "You've still got a stamina that continues to surprise me. Get some rest, little girl. I'll take guard."

"Wake me in thirty minutes if Fawke isn't back." I wouldn't sleep until he returned, but I could sit and get off my feet.

Fawke returned in twenty-eight minutes. "On your feet. Found a place, but we have to hurry. The army has passed, but the manhole isn't hidden. A helicopter will easily spot us."

We scrambled up and squeezed back through the maze of concrete. Fawke pointed out the area where the manhole was. Not far, but wide open. There'd be no hiding.

We dashed for the hole he'd left open, half climbing, half jumping to the sewer floor. A Malignant lay at the bottom of the ladder.

"I had a visitor," Fawke said. "Thankfully, only one." He slid the grate back into place. "There are two more manholes between here and the army camp. One opens right at the fence. Let's head back and take another direction." He wrote in chalk our location. "We won't stop again until nightfall."

As we traveled, we'd hear the jeeps overhead. When we passed grates, the thump of the helicopters, the occasional order shouted. The sounds faded the further we went.

When the sounds of the army no longer broke the silence, Fawke would climb up each ladder we came to, survey the area, then make a note. On and on we went, turning each corner like the rats that swarmed at our feet.

Where were all the Malignants? Had we killed

the only group that knew of the tunnels? Why weren't they in the sewers feasting on the horde of rodents? Were the soldiers easily targeted? The beasts had no more need of going underground because of the soldiers and their garbage. Question after question whirled through my head. The continuous march gave me nothing more to do other than put one foot in front of the other and think.

"Here," Fawke said, from the top of the ladder. "We're a short distance from the field. We can take cover in the tall weeds until morning."

We moved several yards out and bedded down. A clear sky promised no rain. Cold from the ground seeped through my clothes. I wrapped my arms around me in an attempt to keep warm.

Fawke moved close and lay next to me, pulling me against his chest. "I'll keep you warm. Go to sleep, Crynn." His breath tickled my hair. "I'd kiss you if we weren't wearing these riot masks, but I started to take mine off and gagged. We all reek." His chuckle rumbled through his chest.

I smiled and closed my eyes, falling asleep in the warmth and safety of his arms, only to be shaken awake sometime later. "What?"

"Get up." Fawke tossed me my pack. "They've set the field on fire."

"How'd they know we were here?" Smoke rose from the weeds on the edge.

"Nowhere else to look, I guess."

I froze at the sound of crackling flames coming closer.

19

I froze for only a second before fleeing across the field away from the hungry blaze consuming the field. The far-off city was too great a distance. I pointed to an old concrete building that looked more like a bunker.

Fawke shook his head and veered horizontal to the flames. "Find a way through, then into a manhole. We'll never reach a building in time."

Heat licked at my back, smoke burned my lungs. Coughing, I followed Fawke, trusting him, once again, to get me out of danger. Tears flowed from my eyes. The riot shield prevented me from wiping them away. I tried to blink away the smoke so the tears would stop to no avail.

"I can't see!"

Fawke grabbed my hand and pulled me through an opening in the flames. Several more got through before the fire closed. "Keep running. Find another opening. Lead them, Ezra."

Ezra gave a grave nod and increased his pace.

With my heart in my throat, I cast glances at most

of my comrades in a race for their life. Breathless, I slipped from Fawke's grasp.

"Come on, Crynn. We'll die if we stop." He gripped my hand again.

Sheer fear spurred me on.

Dante and Kira leaped over the flames.

Ezra darted through where a patch of concrete had stopped the flames, leading Gage and a few others to our side. He waved those left behind to keep going. "Follow us." He pointed in the direction we ran where a concrete culvert beckoned like a path to freedom.

Dirt kicked up at my feet. When it happened again, I glanced over my shoulder, spotting a sniper on the nearest building. "Fawke!"

"I see him. Keep going. Get to that culvert."

A man cried out. I looked back to see him fall, only to be consumed by the fire. His screams rose over the crackling of the flames. When Kira paused, I called for her to keep going. She grabbed the firing weapon the man had dropped and followed.

We dove into the culvert and sprinted to our left. If not for Fawke keeping hold of my hand, I'd have fallen. His willpower and strength kept me going. That and the fear of being burned alive.

He led us into what had once been a water drainage system leading to the sewers and stopped at the end. "We jump from here."

I stared at a ten-foot drop. The rank odor let me know we'd come to another sewer entrance. I nodded and jumped, tucking into a roll to lessen the impact. The landing still jarred my teeth.

All around me, others took the leap and rolled,

following mine and Fawke's example. "Anyone hurt?" I asked.

Heads shook as they scrambled to their feet.

"Keep going," Fawke said. "We aren't safe yet."

On we ran, not stopping until we came to a ladder leading to the top. Fawke climbed up, looked around, and waved us up.

I came out in the middle of a cleared street. Across from us was the building being rebuilt by the army. The sound of hammering came from inside the building. "We're too close."

"We're right where I want to be. They won't expect us to be right next door. Stay low. Stay quiet."

We raced toward the fallen building next door and into darkness. Fawke dropped his pack.

"You've balls of steel, man." Ezra clapped him on the shoulder.

"Get some rest," Fawke said quietly. "I'll keep watch for an hour, then wake someone to take my place."

I collapsed to the floor, drawing in a huge lungful of air. Exhaustion kept my mind from whirling of the possible dangers of being so close to the army and sent me straight to sleep.

I'd expected to be woken to relieve Fawke and was surprised when I woke to silence and nightfall. My stomach rumbled, and my throat begged for water. Sitting up, I noticed everyone else sitting quietly eating military rations. After the day we'd had, we needed more sustenance than a dry bar of rat and vegetables.

"Hello, sleepy head." Fawke sat next to me.

"You should have woken me." I pulled out a

ration. "Did you get any sleep?"

"Yes. Between Ezra, Moses, and Dante, we all got plenty."

"What now?"

"Back to the sewers. It's the safest place. Hopefully, the army will think we perished in the fire."

I nodded. "They saw us run from the field. Shot at us."

"The fire could have overtaken us." He shrugged, frowning. "We've nowhere else to go but back to the compound. Is that what you want to do?"

"I'd rather know all the exits out of the sewers. Then, I want to see what's in that other city."

He chuckled. "Can we at least rest a while before that mission?"

I smiled. "I'll give you a few days."

Once I'd eaten, he called for the others to gather their things. "We need to be underground before the soldiers wake up."

"Want to steal some of their things?" Gage asked.

"No. I don't want them to know we were here." He peered out the entrance, then waved us forward.

Another dash across the street, then down into the sewers. "It's starting to rain," the last woman in said. "My hand burns."

"Here." Kira dug some salve from her pack, smeared it on the burn, then wrapped clean gauze around her hand. "One drop won't kill you."

But a deluge would, and that's what started pouring in, running off the street like a waterfall. I grabbed the bag hanging on my belt. "Rubber suits. Now." I'd long since given up modesty and stripped from my riot gear to pull on the rubber suit. Being a Stalker, constantly surrounded by the rest of your team, left no room for privacy. If I wanted privacy, I had to stay at the compound.

"Y'all okay?" Lars's voice came through my earpiece.

"Where have you been? We've been shot at, almost burned to death, we could've used your guidance." I rattled off the words.

"Technical difficulties. One of the new kids got fascinated with the control panel and played with some things. We're back up."

"Did Sonny's group ever show up?"

"Yep. All squared away."

"We're back in the sewers. It's raining harder than I've ever seen."

"Yes, it's obscuring the cameras. Be careful. Sharon has called a few times, but Jenkins takes care of things."

Water started to pool at my feet. I hung up and glanced around the group, noting the fear on their faces. "Let's go. The suits will protect you." If the water didn't rise too high. If it did, it might seep between the bodysuit and the hood.

We moved quickly away from the manhole. With so many places for the rain to come in, the water continued to increase. The worry lines on Fawke's face did not fill me with confidence.

By now the water reached my knees. "It didn't rain like this last winter."

"The weather seems to be changing," Fawke said. "It always rains in the winter, but you're right. Not like this. We've got to get out of here, but up top isn't safe either."

"We keep going?"

"Until the water rises too high."

I sighed heavily and continued trudging after him while the water continued to rise. Since I was the shortest there, the water rose up me faster. When it reached my waist, I wanted no more of it. "I'll take my chances up top. It's getting hard for me to move. If I fall…"

Fawke glanced back and nodded. "Up we go. We won't have to worry about Malignants, but the army has ponchos. Hopefully, they'll still hold up somewhere. We'll find a place out of the rain. Once it stops, the water will run into that culvert and out of the sewers."

Back on street level, we splashed our way to a sagging awning, then into a bomb-blasted room. Hours later, the rain still poured and ran down the sides of the street like small rivers.

"Anyone out and about, Lars?" I asked.

"Not that I can tell. Man, it's bad out there."

"Says the man safely in the underground compound."

He laughed. "I'll stay glued to the monitor."

I lay back against my pack and drank some water. Funny how it covered the outside, but the only water safe to drink was what we carried in our packs. At least the compound had the purification center. The people were safe. Us, on the other hand, only time would tell. I felt as if we'd been traveling and running for weeks instead of days.

"Might as well catch up on rest," Fawke said. "No telling how long this rain will last."

Lightening flashed. Thunder roared overhead. The storm was too close for comfort. I glanced up, thankful no bars extended high into the sky.

"Well, the last couple of days have been a real yahoo," Ezra said. "Soldiers, a fire, Malignants, now a downpour of rain that can kill you. No boredom here."

"Are you bored at home?" Gage arched a brow. "I like doing nothing more than training kids and hanging out with the latest man to catch my eye. Sure beats this." She waved a hand.

Fawke sent me an amused glance, knowing that I was torn between adventure and routine. I'd never asked him what he preferred.

"What about you?" I tilted my head.

"I'm happy wherever you are."

My face heated at the truth in his words. Since my arrival and finding out his sole purpose as a Stalker was to protect the leader, he'd remained by my side. Soon wanting to be with me outshined duty. I wanted it no other way.

I knew what I wanted the future to hold. An end to Soriah and a life with Fawke. Not one of running and killing, but one of love and family. Someday, we'd sit down and discuss that future.

I leaned into him, taking comfort from his solid strength, and listened to the friendly conversations of my comrades. They spoke of everything from meals to families to what they wanted to see in a world without Soriah.

"I want the freedom to be a doctor," Kira said. "To get the training without a wheel deciding my fate."

"Married with kids." Samson gave a nod. "That sounds like heaven to me."

"Why get saddled down?" Jolt, the last Stalker to arrive before we revolted, shook his head. "We get new girls arriving all the time. I'm playing the field."

The same age as me, he seemed years younger. "You keep on breaking hearts. One day, you'll find yours shattered."

"No way, Crynn. I'm not made to be a one-woman man."

The group laughed, the scene almost like a party, while rain poured in a steady stream from the awning. Let them relax. We were safe enough here. At least until the rain stopped, and we ventured back out.

My mind drifted to the city across the field I was certain no longer burned. Not in this downpour. Had they seen the fire? The smoke? Were they close enough to hear the guns when they went off? Did they wonder about us?

"What's on your mind?" Fawke asked softly. "You seem miles away."

"I am. I'm thinking about the other city, and wishing the tunnels went that far so we wouldn't have to cross in the open."

"An awful long way to dig."

"Which is why it's a silly thing to wish." I turned so his arms could wrap me from behind. "I like the sound of the rain and thunder. It's peaceful here."

"I like holding you like this."

"Flirt." I smiled even as I wished he wouldn't hold me at a mental arm's length. Why not love each other even during these uncertain times? He knew how I felt, how he felt, but saying the words made him vulnerable. There was no understanding this man sometimes.

I jerked to a sitting position and grabbed my firing weapon as a jeep stopped outside our hiding place.

20

I crawled to where I could see out. The jeep sat still, no sign of the soldiers emerging into the rain. "What do we do?"

"We could disable the jeep," Dante suggested. "I could sneak around behind it and toss in a bomb."

Fawke scratched his neck. "Too loud. Maybe they'll move on."

"Maybe they won't." I lowered my gun, keeping my gaze on the jeep. "We're stuck in here if they don't. Our weapons are no match for the jeep's gun."

The jeep sat there after the rain stopped, not moving on until nightfall. No soldiers ever exited the machine.

When it passed out of sight, we splashed through puddles and back to the sewers. The water had receded to my ankles, making walking easier.

Fawke stopped suddenly as we rounded a corner and raised his weapon.

"Don't shoot. I want to come."

I peered around Fawke to see a soldier push away from the wall.

"Were you in that jeep?"

"Yeah. Snuck out while the other two took a nap. I knew you guys couldn't be far. I'm armed and ready to fight."

"Why?" I stepped from around Fawke.

"You must be the girl that has the city in such an uproar. Rumor is you're dead."

"Doesn't appear that way. If you're wanting to head to our safe place, you'll be disappointed. We've days still before we've mapped all the sewers." By then, we'd know whether or not we could trust this man.

"No worries. Name is Jerod." His gaze flicked to Gage who grinned through her shield.

I rolled my eyes. "Any knowledge of the sewers?"

"Just close to the camp. I'm guessing the commander might have a map, though. But, I'm not going back for it. I'm too pretty to have my head on a stake."

"Let's go." Fawke marched past him, leaving the soldier to step next to Gage.

I guessed he'd be her flavor of the month.

We spent the night wading through sludge while Fawke went up and down ladders marking the locations. It wasn't until the sky turned to gray instead of black that he came down grinning. "We're at the base of the wall that surrounds Soriah."

"We've done it." I sagged against the damp wall of the sewer. "We've found a way to get close."

"Now what?" Moses asked. "We aren't ready to formulate an attack."

"No, but we're a lot closer than we were. Now,

we head back. It's time." I glanced at Fawke who nodded.

It took almost four days for us to reach the compound. When we got close, we blindfolded Jerod.

"Why?" He backed up.

"We don't know if you're trustworthy or not."

He frowned. "Of course, I am. I put my life at risk tracking you down."

Which worried me. He'd found us too easily for my taste. "It's blindfold or die."

He cursed and turned around, complaining when Ezra tied the scarf too tight around his eyes.

"Hand on my shoulder, you poor baby." Ezra put the man's hand on his shoulder. "Don't let go. You'll get lost down here by yourself." He removed the blindfold when we left the sewer and entered the tunnels.

"Wow." Jerod glanced around. "This is amazing. You live down here?"

"Nearby. We're using the tunnels to expand." I tapped my earpiece. "Lars?"

"Got you, boss."

"Tunnels clear?"

"You'll run into a small group of Malignants in about an hour. They're sleeping so shouldn't be too hard to dispose of. I'll alert you when you're close. Who's the grunt?"

"Deserting soldier."

Lars clicked off, coming back on an hour later. "Monsters around the next corner. Two adults, three juveniles. All sleeping."

Fawke had most of the group hold back, taking

me and Ezra with him. "Quick and quiet."

We moved slowly to the group huddled against a tunnel wall and disposed of them with our swords before calling the others. Jerod's eyes widened. "I've never seen one of those things this close up before. They really stink."

"About as much as we do." I couldn't wait for a shower.

Jenkins opened the door as we approached, eyeing Jerod with suspicion, but not saying anything. "Whoa." He gagged and backed up. "You smell like you've been in a toilet."

"We have." Ezra pounded on the man's back. "What fun. Should've been there."

I laughed. "Meet us in the dining room after we've cleaned up." After dropping my weapons and suits in the armor to be cleaned and put away, I headed straight for the shower. After the deluge we'd had, I didn't need to worry about a shortage of water. The river would be rushing.

I adjusted the temperature to just below how hot I preferred to make sure the others had hot water and stepped under the flow. We'd found a way to get close to Soriah! I danced a little jig under the shower spray. It hadn't been easy, but we'd done it.

Once I showered off the grime and dressed in simple clothes, I joined Fawke and Jenkins in the dining room. The rest of our group sat at different tables, now clean and filling their bellies. Jerod looked shell-shocked. I smiled, doubting he expected to find we lived as well as we did.

"What's up?" Jenkins crossed his arms and leaned back in his chair.

"We found another city."

He straightened, bringing all four legs of the chair to the floor with an echoing bang. "Say that again."

"It's a few days march, but once we got to the edge of this city, we saw smoke rising among the ruined buildings of another. If they'll join us, we'll have our army. Oh, and we can get close to Soriah through the sewers."

"Your mission was a great success then."

I nodded, accepting a plate of food from my mother. "Thanks. I told you I'd be back."

She patted my head. "I prayed you would be. Eat. We'll talk later."

"Lock me up." Jerod approached our table with his hands out.

"What for?" I frowned.

"I was ordered to infiltrate your group as a deserter, then alert the army where you take me."

"You can't do that. You don't know how to get here." I continued eating.

"Listen."

I glanced up, arching a brow. "You thought we lived worse than the army. That we were nothing more than ruthless killers. Now, you've seen this place, the women and children, and realized we are far better off than the army. Am I right?"

He nodded. "I lied to you."

"You aren't the first. Go back to your table."

"You're not going to lock me up?"

"Why should I? You've made your choice. Welcome to Rebel City. Got any skills?" I popped a bite of carrot into my mouth.

"I used to be an electrician."

"Then we can use you." After he returned to the table, I glanced at Fawke and burst into laughter. "He reminded me of a child I'd seen once confess to stealing a cookie."

"His lie was far worse, but I'm sure we can trust him now."

"If only he could tell others how it is here without divulging our location." I pushed away my empty plate. "When do you want to head to the other city?"

"Give us a week to rest," Fawke said. "Then we'll go introduce ourselves."

"Sounds good to me."

Lloyd, Jenkins's right-hand man rushed to our table with a metal winged contraption. "Do you know what this is?" He could barely contain his excitement. "It's a drone. We have three."

"Do they work?" I bolted to my feet. "Jerod!"

The ex-soldier hurried toward us. "Yeah?"

"Are you familiar with these things?"

"Sure. I've built them before. This is a really old model, but it'll do the job of filming or taking pictures."

"Where did you find them?" Fawke took the drone and studied it.

"We're still going through all those containers Eb had. I can't wait to open the last few."

"This is a great find." I nodded. "Jerod, get them working. Lloyd will show you where to get the tools you need." I didn't know much about drones, but if we could "see" that far off city before setting off for it, that would be amazing.

Three days later, Jerod handed me a working

drone. "Took a while to figure out this late model, but I've flown it around the halls. The children thought it the greatest thing and chased it. Ready for a test flight to that city? It's fully charged and the battery will last two days."

"How long to get it there?"

"An hour." He grinned. "These things are fast."

"Is the door cleared, Jenkins?"

"Yep. Cleared and disguised. You won't have to step out to release that thing, just open the door."

"Once it's out, we'll be able to watch what it records on the camera monitors," Jerod said. "Wasn't hard to link."

I smiled at Fawke. "Ready?"

"More than ready." He took my hand and headed for the exit door.

Jerod stepped up to the door and opened it. With a push of the button on the controller he held, the drone rose into the sky and zipped away.

Like children receiving a special gift, we slammed the door closed and raced to the control room. The drone picked up everything. The shattered buildings, the cleared roads, the half-burned field as it sped to the city in the distance.

The closer the drone got, the faster my heart beat. Soon, in minutes, we'd know whether the city truly was inhabited by humans and or Malignants. When we decided to head that way, we'd have a better idea of what to expect. My grip tightened on Fawke's.

"Slow it down," I said as the drone passed the first building.

The drone slowed. The city looked much as the one we lived in had before the army's improvements, minus the gas fires.

Some Malignants glanced up as the drone flew overhead. From their open mouths, I was pretty sure they shrieked at this new intruder.

"There. Get closer." I'd spotted something moving in the shadows.

The drone lowered, getting closer. It hovered over the shocked face of a young man.

There were others.

www.cynthiahickey.com

Multi-published and best-selling author, Cynthia Hickey, writing as Cynthia Melton, has taught writing at many conferences and small writing retreats. She and her husband run the publishing press, Winged Publications, which includes some of the CBA's best well-known authors. They live in Arizona and Arkansas, becoming snowbirds with two dogs and one cat. They have ten grandchildren who them busy and tell everyone they know that "Nana is a writer."

Connect with me on FaceBook
Twitter
Bookbub
Sign up for my newsletter and receive a free short story
www.cynthiahickey.com

Follow me on Amazon

Fantasy
Fate of the Faes
Shayna
Deema
Kasdeya

Fate of the Faes boxed set

Dystopian
The Wheel
The Hunt

www.ingramcontent.com/pod-product-compliance
Lightning Source LLC
Chambersburg PA
CBHW070304120726
47910CB00007B/2369